**DO NOT REMOVE
CARDS FROM POCKET**

UNCLE COMANCHE

UNCLE COMANCHE

J. A. Benner

A Chaparral Book

Fort Worth: Texas Christian University Press

Copyright © 1996, Judith Ann Benner

Library of Congress Cataloging-in-Publication Data

Benner, J. A. (Judith Ann), 1942-
    Uncle Comanche / by J. A. Benner.
        p. cm. — (Chaparral book for young readers)
    Summary: In Texas in the 1840s, young Sul Ross runs away from home and,
joining up with his friend Sergeant Hanse Mason, visits a friendly Comanche village, rescues a ferry passenger from a flood, and is invited to run the ferry and study
with the school teacher, the widow of the former ferry owner.
    ISBN 0-87565-152-6 (pbk. : alk. paper)
    1. Ross, Lawrence Sullivan, 1838-1898—Juvenile fiction.
[1. Ross, Lawrence Sullivan, 1838-1898—Fiction. 2. Comanche Indians—Fiction.
3. Ferries—Fiction. 4. Texas—Fiction.]
I. Title. II. Series.
PZ7. B4355Un 1996
[Fic]—dc20   95-36530
                                                                              CIP
                                                                              AC

The text for Uncle Comanche *was designed by A. T. Row.*
The cover illustration is by Dana Adams.

Contents

Ferry Across the Brazos   1

A Special Guest   5

Plans   15

Riding for a Fall   25

Red Rover   35

To the Woodshed   43

What Would Napoleon Do?   51

Runaway   59

On the Trail   69

Ride the Man Down   77

On the Plains   85

Comanches   93

Captured   103

At the Village of the People   111

He-Who-Sees-Far   119

Knife in the Dark   129

Heading Home   139

Flood at Barton's Ferry   147

To the Rescue   153

A Door Opens   161

Lawrence Sullivan "Sul" Ross   167

Glossary   171

Selected Readings   173

For Chris,
who wanted more

FERRY ACROSS THE BRAZOS

There had been a slight rise on the Brazos River that May morning in 1850, and by midafternoon the muddy current was tugging steadily at the little ferry crossing between the village of Waco and the river's east bank. But eleven-year-old Lawrence Sullivan Ross handled the ropes and pulleys expertly in spite of the increased current, using his wiry strength to bring the small, flat-bottomed craft skillfully to the Waco landing.

"Bye, Mr. Petry," the boy called, tying up as a horseman rode past him off the ferry. "Glad you had a good trip."

"Thanks for the smooth crossing, Sul." The rider checked his mount long enough to toss the boy a five-cent piece. "That's for yourself," the man said as he headed his horse up the steep bank toward the village at the top. "See you again soon."

Sul Ross dug into the pocket of his homespun britches and, pulling out a handful of coins, counted them. Two dollars and seventy-five cents...three dollars and ten cents...with the extra five cents, three dollars and fifteen cents. Sul grinned to himself and nodded so sharply that his black curls danced. "Just wait until I tell Pete," he said to himself. "The last time he worked the ferry, he only took in fifty cents!"

His blue eyes sparkling in his delight at beating his older brother's most recent take, Sul shoved the coins back into his britches pocket and glanced both ways to see if there were any more possible customers for the ferry. There were none, and he drew a cooked sweet potato from his dinner pail and pulled a small book—a life of Napoleon written for boys—from the pocket of his hickory shirt. Perching cross-legged on a keg on the ferry landing, the boy bit into the sweet potato and opened his book.

Fascinated by the story, Sul read for some time; then a long shadow suddenly fell across the page, and he looked up to find his tall, formidable father looming over him.

"Haven't I told you about wasting time when you have a job to do?" Shapley Ross demanded angrily. "Give me that book!" He held out one hand.

Sul hesitated, knowing his father was capable of throwing the book into the river while in a fit of temper. "Please be careful with it, Pa," he begged, getting down from the keg. "It belongs to Mr. Battle."

"The schoolmaster?" the frontiersman asked. "Then what are you doing with it?"

"He loaned it to me because I was asking him questions about Napoleon," Sul explained. "He knows I want to be a soldier."

His father ignored his last statement. "Let me see the book," he ordered. When the boy reluctantly handed him the biography, his father glanced into it. "At least you aren't reading something silly like poetry," Shap Ross admitted grudgingly. "But you know how I feel about schoolwork—it's to be done at school or at home after supper. Right now you've got the ferry to run."

"But there's nobody wanting to cross right now," Sul pointed out reasonably. "I would have heard them if they had wanted the ferry."

"Well, you sure didn't hear me." Shapley Ross snorted. "Why are you reading now, anyway?"

"It helps to pass the time—and gives me something to think about while waiting. At least I'm not *wasting* time, Pa."

"That remains to be seen." His father snorted again and flicked the book cover with one fingernail. "All right, you can read Mr. Battle's book, but the first time you fail in doing your job here, I'll tan your hide so that you won't be able to sit down for a week. You understand?"

Sul nodded and took back the book. "Yes, Pa. And thank you."

Shapley Ross waved away his thanks. "What kind of take have you made this afternoon?"

"More than three dollars—three fifteen to be exact." Sul passed the money over and watched while his father counted it.

"For a boy who doesn't like arithmetic, I'm glad to know you can be trusted with money," the elder Ross said, and Sul beamed at this praise. Shap Ross put the change into a money pouch and pulled the thong tight. "I'm going out to the farm to check on Sweetbriar," he said, pocketing the pouch. "There's a rise on the river, so be careful. You do remember what I told you about *that*, don't you?"

Sul nodded. "You said a heavy rain above us could send a flood down the river and capsize the ferry. I'm to look at the current and listen good for the sound of rushing water before I cross."

"Well, you've got that down pat, all right," his father admitted. "Just be sure you remember it."

"I will," Sul promised.

As the elder Ross started back up the bluff, he turned to his son once more. "Pete will be coming to spell you when he gets home from tutoring."

"Aw, Pa, does he have to?" Sul asked. "I like operating the ferry."

"You've got extra chores to do at home," his father reminded him. "Your mother needs your help more now that Pete's being tutored."

Sul wrinkled his nose. "I know—algebra and geometry and Latin and French. But I already know more about French than Pete does. Ma's a good teacher, and I've picked it up just listening to her helping Pete at night."

Shap Ross frowned at this boast, and Sul decided his father was not impressed. "If you're really so smart," the elder Ross said, "you should be the one to help your mother this evening. She's got that big party for your sisters coming up, and Pete needs to study while he waits for ferry passengers."

The boy blinked and swallowed hard at this news. "Yes, Pa," he said. "But I can keep operating the ferry while Pete's busy, can't I? I did make all that money this afternoon."

"As long as you don't skylark around and lose money for us, you can," Shapley Ross agreed.

As Sul watched his father stride back up the road to the settlement, he considered his position in the family. He learned more quickly than Pete, made friends more easily, and was always his father's choice to ride the family's entries in the local horse races. In fact, he was more like his father in many ways—except for appearance—than his older brother.

Sul sighed. "If only I looked more like Pa!" he told himself. Sadly, the boy considered the unfairness of life. Pete had been named for their mother's side of the family, but he looked like his father and the Rosses. He, Sul, on the other hand, had been named for the Rosses but looked like his mother's people. It hardly seemed just.

"Why couldn't I have been Pa's favorite son?" he asked himself. "Then maybe I could take special schooling instead of having to do extra chores." Pete didn't like to study—or to read either. Sul sighed again, enviously, at the thought of all the new books his brother would get to read. He picked up a stone and threw it as far as he could into the mainstream current of the Brazos. "It's just not fair," he said out loud.

A SPECIAL GUEST

At the distant rattle of a buggy across the river, Sul looked up. Shading his eyes with one hand, he tried to identify the horse and driver. Finally he decided that the gray between the shafts could only be Lady Jane, a new racer belonging to a farmer who lived several miles out the Dallas road. At the last Waco racing meet, the Ross family's entry with Sul in the saddle had lost to Lady Jane by a nose, but the boy knew that in racing there was always a next time. With a grin of anticipation, Sul went to meet the call of "Ferry!"

"I'll be right over!" he shouted, and the driver of the buggy raised his whip to show he had heard. Stepping onto the ferry, Sul leaned over the side to study the current. A quick glance told the boy that the rate of the river's flow was about the same as it had been the last time he crossed, and when he listened there were no unusual water sounds. Judging it safe, Sul untied the mooring lines and threw his strength into jerking the rope and pulley arrangement which would take the ferry to the other side.

The rig was waiting at the other landing when the ferry glided in. "Hi, Mr. Jonas," Sul called, tying up. "Bring her on board."

He waited for the driver to move his rig forward, but the mare had other ideas. Snorting nervously, she balked at setting foot on the deck.

"What's the matter with you?" her owner asked, raising his whip. "Get along there!" He flicked her with the lash and the mare started and plunged forward, dragging the buggy on board. Her shod hoofs slipped on the deck; frightened, she reared and almost fell. The ferry rocked dangerously.

"Don't do that!" Sul yelled. "She could turn us over!" He leaped for the mare's head, grabbing her reins just below the bit and pulling her head down. "Easy, Lady Jane. Easy, girl," he soothed, and the wild scrabbling calmed. "Don't hit her, Mr. Jonas," he begged. "She'll be all right if you don't frighten her again. A lot of horses balk at first." He reached out to pat the mare's neck. To his great satisfaction, the gray dropped her head and stood quietly.

The mare's owner laughed nervously. "Could she really have turned us over?" he asked.

"That's what Pa said," Sul answered, going to cast off.

"I'll say this for you, Sul," the farmer said when they had started back across the river, "you can handle horses better than anybody I've ever seen. Better than your pa even, and that's sayin' somethin'."

The boy grinned at this compliment and turned from working the ferry ropes to stroke the gray's nose lovingly. "As soon as I turn twelve, Pa's going to take me to Houston to race. She's a fine mare, Mr. Jonas. I'd like to race her for you sometime."

"If your pa can spare you from ridin' his own horses maybe you can. But why aren't you in school?" the farmer asked, handing over his fare. "And where's Pete? I haven't seen much of him lately."

Sul grinned again as he pocketed the coins. "With summer coming on, I get out at noon nowadays." His eyes sparkled. "And since Pete's taking special schooling, I get to work the ferry."

"What kind of special schoolin' is that?"

"Oh, silly stuff like Latin and French and mathematics." The boy's tone was scornful.

"What's your pa goin' to do — make a lawyer out of Pete?"

Sul shrugged as the ferry moved into midstream. "I only know I want to be a soldier — or a ranger."

"Well, you'll make a good one," Jonas said.

"I want to be the best," the boy said. He looked up at the older man. "Mr. Jonas, what do you know about Bonaparte?"

"Not much. Is he your hero?"

Sul shook his head so sharply his curls danced again. His round face puckered in distress at the memory of what he had just read. "He left his army to suffer on the retreat from Moscow and hurried back to Paris. That's why I asked — I hoped you could tell me why he'd do that when his troops loved him."

They were coming into the landing now, and Jonas laughed as he took up his whip. "Lord, Sul, I don't know. Ask your pa."

"Pa wouldn't know — he doesn't like history."

"Then ask a soldier," Jonas suggested. "There's plenty of men around here who served in Mexico."

"That's a good idea," Sul agreed. He waved as his passenger drove away. As soon as he was sure his services would not be needed any time shortly, he whipped out the book and plunged back into the story.

He was still reading sometime later when a sound from the road made him look up. Sul saw Pete come striding the last few yards down the bank, his new jacket slung over one shoulder.

As his brother approached, Sul eyed him closely. Pete was only two years older than he was, but already he was inches taller. Even with his lighter brown hair, Pete Ross looked more like their father every day.

"Does Pa know you're wasting your time reading?" the older boy asked as he stepped onto the landing.

Sul deliberately closed the book and faced Pete. As long as he could remember, his older brother had been set to keep him in line. "What are you going to do — run to him and snitch?" he asked. "I'll pound you if you do."

Pete went red, but he kept his temper. "As if you could," he said. "Besides, you'll get a hiding from Pa if you try. These are my good clothes."

Sul looked him up and down, considering if he dared start a fistfight. At last he decided to let the incident pass. "Pa already knows. He said I could read as long as I don't neglect the ferry."

Pete tossed his jacket onto a nearby bench. "Well, for now Ma says to hurry home. Company's come for supper, and she wants you there."

Sul went to get his own gear. "Who is it — Mr. Coke?" he asked hopefully.

"Better than that," Pete said.

Sul considered who would be a better guest than lawyer Dick Coke with his stories of Virginia. "George Barnard?" he asked.

"George stopped by last night after you'd gone to bed. You know he's courting Mary."

"Well, who is it then?" Sul asked impatiently.

Pete grinned. "This visitor wears a uniform."

Sul's face brightened. "Hanse? Hanse is here?"

Pete Ross nodded. "He just rode in. And you should call him Sergeant Mason," he corrected.

Sul ignored his brother's bossy attitude. "But we've always called Hanse by his first name," he protested. "Why the sudden change?" His eyes narrowed suspiciously. "You've sure been acting uppity lately. What's going on, anyway?"

"I've got my reasons," Pete said smugly, and Sul saw his brother's eyes gleaming like they did when he knew something to his own advantage. "Who crossed last?"

The distraction worked. "Mr. Jonas," Sul replied. "He said I could handle a horse better than anybody he'd ever seen — "

"You shouldn't tell that on yourself," Pete interrupted him. "You know what Hanse always said about bragging."

Stung by this reminder, Sul answered heatedly. "So you call him 'Hanse,' too, you hypocrite."

"I'm not calling him that any more to his face," Pete said loftily. "And I certainly never called him anything as silly as 'Uncle Comanche.' Don't you know by now he doesn't like to be called 'Comanche'? It makes people think he's a half-breed."

Angered by Pete's attitude, Sul again considered giving his brother a well-deserved pounding. He clenched his fists and stepped forward.

"Don't try it," Pete warned. "I can still lick you."

With an effort, Sul brought his temper under control. He returned the book on Napoleon to his shirt pocket. "I'm going home," he announced, picking up his dinner pail and starting up the bank. "As for Hanse," he told Pete over his shoulder, "other people called him 'Comanche.' How was I to know the difference? He never told me not to." Farther up the road, he stopped and cupped his hands around his mouth. "Maybe I called Hanse 'Uncle Comanche,'" he hollered, "but at least I don't have to be tutored!" Then he turned and sprinted up the road to the family cabin at the top of the bluff. He was almost home before he realized he had forgotten to tell Pete of the fares he had collected that day.

As he approached the Ross cabin, Sul slowed to a sedate walk in case their visitor was watching. When he was little, he would have rushed without a thought to climb onto his hero's knee. Now that he was going on twelve years old he wouldn't run to meet an older friend, even if that friend was a sergeant in the Dragoons and had lived with the Comanches as a boy.

Coming around the corner of the double log cabin, Sul met his oldest sister, Mary, on the dogtrot. She had just finished milking and was bringing a pail of fresh milk inside.

"Where's Ma?" he asked casually, setting his dinner pail down on the porch.

"Inside finishing supper, but we're going to eat out under the trees tonight," his sister told him. "In case you're wondering, Hanse is with her."

Sul grinned at this news and started for the nearest door, only to find his sister blocking his way.

"Ma said you were to wash up as soon as you came in," Mary told him, with all the authority of her eighteen years. She indicated a washstand on the gallery. "There's a comb there, too. You'd better use it."

Sul grimaced at this bossiness as his sister stepped inside. Still, he went to wash as directed, taking care that he did a thorough job on his face and neck as well as on his arms and hands. If he didn't, he knew his mother or Mary would bring him back out to finish the job themselves, and that would be humiliating. Finally he combed his dampened curls in a vain attempt to smooth them out, but the comb became tangled. As he jerked impatiently at the snarl, Sul wished again that he had wavy brown hair like Pete and his father.

Behind him the cabin door opened. Hoping it wasn't their visitor, Sul turned to find his next oldest sister, Margaret, coming out onto the gallery, the basket she used for picking greens over one arm.

Margaret stopped to watch his struggles. "Let me help you," she said, setting the basket down. Taking the comb from him, she eased it through the tangles. "There," she said with a smile when his curls had finally been arranged to her satisfaction, "now you'll pass inspection."

Sul's eyes flashed. "Curls are sissy," he replied, trying one last time to slick down his hair. Then, schooling himself to a poker face despite the joy and excitement he felt, he entered the cabin.

Hanse Mason was sitting on a bench against the wall, riding

two-year-old Bob, the baby of the family, on his knee and talking to Mrs. Ross when Sul slipped silently in and sat down at the
other end of the bench. On the sergeant's other side sat Mervin,
Sul's six-year-old brother. He coughed hollowly. Mrs. Ross was
working around the big fireplace to finish the last preparations
for supper, but she took time to smile at Sul.

While the boy waited for his friend to notice his arrival, he
studied the sergeant's profile. Sul had known this family friend
as far back as he could remember, for he had been not quite
three when Hanse Mason was first befriended by Shapley and
Catherine Ross after the deaths of his wife and children. Only in
his late twenties now, Hanse looked, in Sul's opinion, much the
same as he always had: muscular and tanned, with straight black
hair and mustache and fierce dark eyes which at times bored
right through you. True to his Comanche upbringing, Mason sel-
dom showed emotion, but when he saw Sul, his harsh features
softened slightly. "Evenin', young'un," he greeted.

"Are you here for long?" Sul asked.

"Only until I can finish some company business. Then I've
got to get back to Fort Graham." Mason paused and turned his
attention to Bob. "That's enough for now, Bobby," he said,
swinging the toddler off his knee and setting him down on the
bench beside him. "You sit there between Sully an' me while
your ma fixes supper." As the sergeant talked, his hands made
the signs for greeting.

To Sul's disgust, Bob immediately let out a howl. "No, mine!"
he said, waving at Hanse and pushing his brother away. Sul
ignored him. Hanse was his friend, but he didn't mind sharing
him. Only a baby, he decided, would be *that* jealous. In reply, he
made the welcome sign.

Mrs. Ross looked up from stirring a big bowl of cornbread bat-
ter. "Margaret," she said to her daughter who had just come in
with the greens for supper, "come take Bob. Hanse has something for your brother, and I must put this in the Dutch oven so

it can start baking." She smiled again at Sul as Margaret snatched up Bob, who only howled louder. "Son, it'll be a while yet until supper. Why don't you take Hanse out to the stable and show him your new racer?"

Sul beamed at his mother's understanding and led Mason outside. "You'll like Saber," he said, speaking of his new horse. "He's a blue roan and mighty fast." Only when they were out on the gallery did he ask, "What did you bring me — another Spanish coin you found?"

"Somethin' better," Mason answered. "Show me your new horse first, an' then I'll let you see it."

Sometime later, when Saber's paces had been displayed and admired and the roan had been returned to his stall, Mason brought out his surprise — a rectangular wooden case — from the blanket roll behind his saddle. "Do you know what this is?" he asked, flipping open the lid to show the boy what was inside.

"A Baby Dragoon Colt," Sul breathed, eyeing the weapon in wonder. The five-shot, smaller model of the army-issue six-shooter was just a boy's size — and the answer to a frontier boy's dream. "Where did you get it, Hanse?"

"Won it in a horse race. Look, it's all here — powder flask, bullet mold, percussion caps, an' everythin'. The fool who wagered it hadn't even fired it yet."

Sul reached out to touch the smooth, satiny wood of the weapon's grips. "It's beautiful," he sighed. "I've shot Pa's regular model, but it's kind of big."

"That's why I brought this for you," the sergeant said, closing the case and handing it to the boy. "Risky as the frontier is, you never know when you'll need a sidearm."

"You're giving it to *me?*" Sul asked, hardly believing his ears. Why, even his good clothes were Pete's hand-me-downs, and the blue roan he was so proud of was actually only his to race for his father.

"That's what I said, wasn't it?" Mason's mouth twisted slightly as if he was about to smile. "You'll have to share it with Pete, but it's really yours, young'un, an' I'll tell your pa so."

"I don't mind sharing," Sul said truthfully after he had somehow managed to speak his thanks. "Could we go try it out?"

Mason shook his head. "Your ma's cornbread should be done about now. Don't worry, there'll be time after supper for us to go shoot it — if you ain't got schoolwork to do."

Sul grimaced. "I do have a spelling test tomorrow I have to study for," he admitted. "But maybe if you talk to Pa, he'll let me go target shooting for a little while."

This time the sergeant actually did smile. "I'll ask your pa to go with us," he said. "Knowin' him, he won't be able to resist shootin' that little beauty himself."

Sul sighed contentedly and hitched up his britches as he walked with Pete downhill toward the river. Supper — especially the cobbler his mother had made in honor of Hanse's visit — had been delicious, and now they were going down to the riverbank to do some target shooting, even as he had hoped. Any other time he would have danced down the bluff, but with Hanse and his father walking behind him, he controlled his excitement and paced sedately, just ahead of the men who had Mervin with them.

As Sul entered the cleared area they always used for target practice, he could hear his father rawhiding Mason about the three helpings of cobbler the sergeant had taken for dessert. The boy grinned at the teasing. It was no secret that Hanse loved Mrs. Ross' cooking.

"If I've learned anythin' from the Comanches an' the army, it's to eat up when good grub's available," Mason answered good-humoredly. "Otherwise it could be a mighty long wait until the next time." He called ahead of them, "You brought that target we fixed up, didn't you, Sully?"

"Right here, Hanse," Pete said, holding up the piece of wooden shingle painted with a bull's-eye.

Sul grinned at Pete's use of Mason's first name. He could tell by his older brother's growing excitement that Pete could hardly wait to shoot the new revolver. "That's all right," the boy told himself. "I didn't expect to get to try it anyway until Pa and Hanse had tired of it." Still grinning, he went to stand with his two brothers behind the firing line while Mason set up the target and his father loaded and capped the revolver.

PLANS

His feet wide apart and his lower lip gripped in his teeth for better concentration, Sul held the Baby Dragoon Colt out at arm's length and thumbed back the hammer. "I told you it throws to the left just a hair," his father, standing behind him, said. "You didn't take that into account your last shot. Let's see you do better this time." To Mason he said, "Toss it up again, Hanse."

Sul nodded. Firing at a stationary mark wasn't enough for Pa's sons — they were expected to hit the bull's-eye on a moving target as well. Gripping his lip tighter, he squinted once more along the sights, waiting for Mason to toss up the shingle. Out of the corner of his eye he could see Mervin squatting by a log and poking at something with a stick.

Then the target flashed upwards. Sul squeezed the trigger. After the little revolver fired, he had the satisfaction of knowing he had hit the shingle. "How was that, Hanse?" he called, lowering the weapon.

Mason stepped forward to pick up the target. "You've done good, young'un. That one was right on center."

"Ya-hoo!" Sul did a happy little victory dance where he stood. "I beat you this time, Pete!" Although Sul was the better horseman, Pete was usually the better shot. To have bested his older brother even once this evening with a new weapon, was, he felt, quite an accomplishment.

Pete grinned at him from his place near Mason. "I'll beat you next round," he promised.

Sul looked back at his father. "Can we shoot another round, Pa?" he asked, ignoring the older man's scowl at his glee in beating Pete.

"One more round, and then we need to get back to the house," Shapley Ross said, going to join Mason. "You and Pete have schoolwork to finish."

Sul nodded again and turned to face the sergeant. He raised the Colt, ready to fire again. Behind him, there was a loud warning buzz.

"Pa! A rattler!" Mervin shrieked. "A big one!"

As one, Sul and his father whirled to face this danger. From where he stood, the boy could see the large diamondback coiled about a foot from Mervin's bare leg. The reptile's head swayed, ready to strike.

Without thinking of anything other than his brother's danger and that he was the closest to do something about it, Sul bounded forward to distract the snake's attention. As he ran up, that wickedly poised head swiveled around to face this new threat. The rattler's tongue flicked rapidly and its rattles buzzed angrily at his approach.

Pausing only long enough to calculate the angle of his shot, Sul stepped as close to the rattler as he dared and squeezed the trigger. As the report echoed and re-echoed between the riverbanks and the powdersmoke burned his nostrils, Sul could only hope that he had not misjudged his aim. That rattler had been too close to Mervin. . . .

As the powdersmoke cleared, he could see the rattler's headless body still writhing belly up on the ground. Beside it, Mervin howled loudly.

Sul pushed the Colt into the waistband of his britches and went to comfort his brother.

"Are you hurt, Merve?" he asked anxiously as his father, Mason, and Pete came running to the spot.

Shap Ross grabbed his older son by the arm. "No thanks to you if he isn't!" he snapped, dragging Sul back. "Don't ever do that again! You could have killed your brother!" Squatting beside Mervin, he said, "Where are you hurt?"

Mervin rubbed one shin with the other leg. "When Sul shot the snake the dirt stung my leg," he whimpered.

Shapley Ross relaxed visibly. "Is that all?" he asked Mervin.

On the other side, Mason knelt beside the youngster for a closer look. "Skin ain't even broken," he told the others. "You're all right, Mervin — thanks to Sully." He nodded approvingly at the older boy.

Shap Ross turned to Sul. "Of all the reckless stunts — Son, you could have been hurt too. A rattler that size can strike almost its full length."

"I know, Pa," Sul said. "That's why I knew I had to kill it before it could strike Mervin. And I did — with one shot, too!"

"It was a good shot, but there's no need to go on about it," Shapley Ross said. He stood and swung Mervin onto his shoulders. "Let's get back to the house, son. It's almost your bedtime."

As Sul followed his father and the others back to the village, he recalled with a blush that Hanse had once told him that a good officer never boasted of saving someone else's life.

Back at the cabin, Shapley Ross set Mervin down and turned to Sul. "Give me your Colt, son," he said, holding out his hand. "I'll clean it and put it away. You've got schoolwork to do."

Sul held back. "But, Pa," he protested, "you and Hanse always taught me to look after my firearms myself. You said I should never depend on another man's cleaning and reloading."

Mason gave a rare laugh. "He's got you there, Shap," the sergeant said. "Let him take care of it before he starts his school-work — I won't let him waste time. Anyway, I need to show him how big a charge of powder to put in them chambers."

Encouraged by this support, Sul looked hopefully at his father.

"All right," Shapley Ross told him, "you can take care of your revolver. But as soon as you finish, you get right in there to work."

Sul grinned. "Thanks, Pa. I will." Starting inside, he said, "I'll get our cleaning kit, Hanse."

"Ask your ma for some hot water," Mason called after him. "We'll need to scald the barrel out as many rounds as we fired tonight."

Sul had cleaned his rifle many times, often with Hanse watching, so he confidently went to work on the Colt. Still, he took special care with his new revolver, scouring out the barrel with hot water to remove the last residue of powder and re-oiling the weapon to prevent rust.

"You ready for inspection?" Mason asked when the boy at last laid down his oiling rag.

Sul handed over the revolver. As the sergeant put the weapon on half cock and spun the cylinder, the boy held his breath, hoping his work would meet Hanse's critical standards.

"Looks good," Mason said finally, and Sul relaxed. "Get your powder flask an' load fifteen grains of powder," the sergeant directed. "Then add your ball an' use the loadin' lever to seat it in the chamber."

Step by step he took the boy through the process of charging each chamber with powder and ball and adding the percussion cap. "There," Mason said when Sul had eased the hammer down out of half-cock position after placing the final cap. "Now you're ready for action again." He smiled slightly at the boy. "You've done enough shootin' to know to keep your powder dry, young'un, but I'm tellin' you to go ahead an' replace your caps too if there's ever any question of 'em bein' damp."

Sul grinned once more and opened the case to put his revolver away. "I won't forget, Hanse," he promised.

Later that evening, Sul sat at the lamp table in the kitchen to do his schoolwork. Across from him, Pete, helped by their mother, struggled with a French assignment from his tutor. Although Sul had his spelling book open to that week's lesson, he could not keep his mind on the words he needed to know for the next day's test.

From where he sat, he could see the case containing his Baby Dragoon Colt on the shelf where his father had placed it. His heart swelled with pride and gratitude as he considered the gift. Thanks to Hanse, he was the luckiest boy in Waco that night.

Sul smiled dreamily, thinking of the feel of the Colt in his hand. Some day he would be a Dragoon like Hanse, using a man's weapon and galloping his cavalry steed into wonderful adventures. Perhaps he could rescue a lost wagon train or blaze a new trail to California. Maybe he could even go to West Point and some day become Captain Sul Ross —

"Aren't you through with those lessons yet?" His father's voice jolted him back to the present. Shap Ross came into the cabin from the gallery and picked up his whiskey jug and a glass. "You'd better snap to it — it's almost your bedtime."

"Almost, Pa," Sul answered, dragging his attention back to the speller. For a while he studied quietly, elbows on the table, chin in hand, feet twisted around the rungs of his chair, but then his mind wandered again. From where he sat he could hear his father and Mason talking on the gallery beyond the open door, and what they were saying was far more interesting than this week's spelling list.

"I've decided to stay in the army," the sergeant was saying.

"Maybe if I knock enough sense into 'em, I can keep some tom-fool greenhorns from gettin' themselves killed by Indians."

"Honestly, though, Hanse," Shap Ross said, "if you had to go live with the Indians again, what would you do? Go look up that band of Comanches who raised you?"

"Been away too long," Mason answered. "No, I'd head up the Brazos to José María's village an' settle there. He's honorable, an' some of them Anadarko gals are plenty good lookin'."

"Marry yourself an Anadarko wife and raise a passel of half-breed brats?" Shapley Ross went on.

"Half-breed young'uns would be better than none," the sergeant said. "But I sure wouldn't want 'em treated the way I've been treated over the years. For a long time you an' your missus were the only folks I knew who didn't act like I was a 'breed."

"Well, I wouldn't have minded having you for a son-in-law," Shap Ross answered. "And I know Sul would have liked to have you in the family." He laughed. "I only wish you wouldn't encourage him, Hanse, by bringing him things like that pocket Colt. I have a hard enough time keeping his mind on his work as it is."

"Mary's better off with George Barnard than she'd be as an enlisted man's wife," Mason replied. "An' as for Sully, I told you before how it was — if that last baby Greta was carryin' had been a boy, he an' Sully would have been the same age. I like to think my boy would have been like your boy, that's all. Sully is — "

Sul never found out what else it was Mason was going to say about him as the clock on the mantel chimed just then. His mother looked up from helping Pete. "Bedtime, son," she said.

Sul stiffened. "Aw, Ma, already? Annie just went to bed, and she's three years younger than I am."

"You've got school tomorrow just like Annie does. And Bob and Mervin have been in bed for hours."

"They're babies, too," Sul said. He closed his speller,

unwrapped his feet, and stood to push his chair under the table. "At least let me say good night to Pa and Hanse."

Mrs. Ross smiled knowingly at him. "Two minutes," she said, "and then you'll have to scoot."

Sul grinned in reply and went outside to say his farewells. He was halfway up the ladder to the boys' sleeping loft when he remembered that he had wanted to ask Hanse about Napoleon.

Up in the loft, close under the shingles, it was still hot as Sul undressed, put on his nightshirt, and climbed into the pallet bed he shared with Pete. Since his brother was allowed to stay up later, he had to sleep on the inside nearest the front cabin wall. Dutifully he crawled to his side of the bed where he plumped up his pillow before stretching out to sleep. But the excitement and lingering heat of the day kept him awake.

For ten or fifteen minutes the boy turned from one side to the other in the hot little loft, listening to his mother and Pete exchanging comments on the French lesson and to the low murmur of talk coming from the front gallery where his father was still entertaining their guest. With a sigh, Sul thought of the cool evening breeze to be found on the porch. Finally he sat up. Near the foot of the bed was a section of the wall where the mud chinking between two of the logs had fallen out. In the winter this gap let in cold air, but tonight it would hopefully provide a needed coolness. Wriggling to the foot of the bed, Sul lay down with his face to the crack and closed his eyes. Cooler air flowed over him, and he began getting sleepy. From outside his father's voice floated up to his listening post.

" — things are looking up. Our farm's doing so-so. The ferry pays well, and the hotel does fine. I've even started a water supply company. Armistead hauls water from the spring to our customers for five cents a bucket. Someday I'm going to build Mrs. Ross a big new house out on our farm — it'll be the talk of the town." Shap Ross' bragging voice grew louder.

The bragging, Sul knew, was a result of the whiskey. Pa usually became boastful if he had had several glasses. Hanse, on the other hand, never drank, not even to be polite.

"Sounds good," Mason said quietly, and suddenly Sul was ashamed of his father's bragging. Hanse never bragged — why, they never would have known he had been cited for bravery at the Battle of Buena Vista by General Zachary Taylor himself if someone else hadn't told them.

"And that's not all," the boy heard Shap Ross go on eagerly. "In a couple of years, or three at the most, I'll have enough put by so I can send Pete back east to military school. After that, I'll have Senator Houston see if he can't get him an appointment to West Point."

Sul's eyes snapped open at this mention of West Point. He rolled over and pressed his left eye and ear to the crack so he could see what his father and Mason were doing and hear what they were saying more clearly.

"What about Sully?" Mason asked casually. "He's got the makin's of an outstandin' cavalry officer. He ain't afraid of nothin', an' he can ride anythin' on four legs."

"Oh, I admit Sul's got plenty of courage," Shapley Ross answered, "but he's too much of a show-off. Look at how he went on about outshooting Pete tonight."

Sul's ears burned. He felt flooded with embarrassment at being branded a show-off. Since Hanse didn't brag, he would have to be more like him and not call attention to his exploits.

Downstairs Hanse spoke up for him. "That's because Sully feels he's got to outdo Pete," Mason told his friend. "I've seen plenty of young officers just like him. Once they figure out we're all on the same side, they do all right."

Shap Ross went on, as if he hadn't heard. "And Sul's reckless. You saw how he went after that rattler without thinking. Granted he did right, but not even the Dragoons want an officer so hotheaded he'll get himself and his men killed. Besides, I doubt that he could plan and carry through a military campaign.

As for West Point — I can't see him going there. For one thing, he hasn't got any talent for mathematics except for counting the ferry take. And you've got to study mathematics at the Point." The frontiersman stretched out his long legs in front of him and jingled the coins in his pockets. "No, Pete's the boy to go into the army. He'll make a fine officer, and with his height he'll look good on a troop horse."

Sul stiffened angrily. He couldn't believe his ears. "Pa is reckless and hotheaded too," he told himself. Why, while in San Antonio during the Mexican War, Pa had threatened to throw a regular army officer into the river when the man had made him angry. "I'm not nearly as hot tempered as Pa!"

"What have you got planned for Sully?" Hanse was asking.

Sul's heart seemed to stand still as he waited for his father to answer Mason's question. When the answer came, it was cheerfully brutal. "The only thing Sul is fit for is to be a farmer," Shap Ross said, "and he's got enough education for that. This is the last year I'll send him to school. Come fall I'll put him to work out on our place."

"An' what if he wants somethin' else?" the sergeant asked.

"He'll get over it," Sul heard his father answer. "When he's old enough, he can take over my farming acreage here." Shapley Ross chuckled. "It won't be so hard on him, Hanse. He likes horses and shows pretty good sense about raising them. And as easy as he makes friends, he can go to the legislature after a while. But Pete will be my West Pointer, yessirree!"

Stunned, Sul could only lie there. His heart pounded in his ears and he felt like he had been kicked by a mule. Become a farmer — when he wanted to be a soldier? And be denied any more education when he loved to read? As for Pete going to West Point — Sul would have laughed if he hadn't been so angry. "Doesn't Pa understand anything about me — or about Pete?" he asked himself. "Pete doesn't want any more schooling. He's having trouble now with that French, Latin, and mathematics tutoring he's getting." Then, with a shock which all but took his breath away, Sul realized that was the reason for Pete's tutoring. Their father had planned for some time to send his brother to the United States Military Academy.

"No wonder Pete's been so uppity lately," Sul moaned. He had known their father's plans while Sul, like a baby, had been left out of them. "He's probably laughing at me right now."

Sul clenched his fists at the thought of Pete's laughter. And it wasn't fair that Pa had decided his future like that, without asking him. "I can be a good officer, I know I can!" he told himself fiercely. "No matter what Pa says, I can plan and carry out a campaign — just like Napoleon!"

Downstairs the party on the gallery was breaking up. A chair scraped on the porch as Shap Ross stood. His voice boomed nearer Sul's listening post. "There's room for you at the hotel, Hanse. I'll walk you over."

"I've known you how long?" the sergeant asked, likewise getting to his feet.

Ross chuckled. "At least since Sul was knee-high. Why?"

"So we've been friends about ten years now," Sul heard Mason continue.

"About that," his father replied.

The sergeant went on. "Well, I'm tellin' you to your face that you're makin' a big mistake about Sully. Send Pete to military school an' try to get him an appointment to West Point if you want, but just remember Sully's got more to him than just bein' a farmer."

Shap Ross laughed again. "I hear you, Hanse, but you're wasting your time. My mind's made up, and I'm not going to change it. Come say good evening to Mrs. Ross before you leave."

Up in the loft, Sul Ross flopped back down at the right end of the bed and punched his pillow angrily. "I'll show you, Pa," he vowed stormily. "I'll show you that you're wrong about everything!"

RIDING
FOR
A FALL

I t was still dark in the cabin when Sul awoke the next morning. For a long time his misery — and resolve — had kept him awake, and he had flopped restlessly even after Pete had come to bed. Sleep, when it had overtaken him, had been troubled and brief. Now, listening to the silent household, he realized he was the first one stirring. And from the sounds the birds were making outside, full dawn was not far off.

With a yawn, Sul sat up in bed. His mind went back to the talk he had overheard the evening before. It still weighed on his heart as though he had an anvil hanging about his neck. "Somehow I've got to prove to Pa that I can be a soldier!" he told himself.

Beside him, Pete mumbled something in his sleep and stirred slightly. He would wake up soon.

Suddenly Sul felt he could not face his brother — not yet. And as for Pa — he certainly didn't want to talk to him. He wanted to slip away from everyone for a while, to come to terms with what his father had said and the plans he had made. A gallop out to the farm and back would be just the thing to lift his spirits. Moving carefully so as not to awaken Pete, Sul crept to the foot of the bed. Usually he gave Pete a brotherly dig in the ribs to remind him of his duties, but this morning he decided to deny himself that pleasure. And if Pete had to be called by Pa to bring in wood and build the breakfast fire, that was his look-out.

Leaving the future West Pointer still sleeping, Sul quietly dressed, including his boots, and made his way down the ladder and outside through the first light to the privy. There had been a rain shower overnight, and the grass in the yard was wet.

When he came out, the first colors of dawn were showing in the clearing sky. Sul pulled up his braces and sprinted for the stable. "If I don't hurry," he told himself, "there won't be time for my chores and a gallop before I have to go to school."

Saber nickered in greeting as the boy slipped into the stable. Closing the door behind him, Sul walked through the building to open the east door leading to the corral. This let in fresh air and light, and in the dimness he could see haltered heads turn. Pete's dun pawed the floor, while across the stable his father's big black horse began to kick the boards of its stall. From a rear stall, Mason's sorrel watched these proceedings hopefully, but Sul knew better than to undertake the responsibility of caring for the sergeant's mount.

"Sorry, boy," he told the sorrel. "Hanse always says a good cavalryman looks after his own horse. He'll want to see to your feeding and grooming himself."

Turning from Mason's horse, Sul considered his own plan. For an instant he thought of leading Saber out there and then, but his training held. On the frontier a man's life often depended upon his horse, and he had been taught to look after his mount before doing anything else. "But we'll have to hurry before Pa shows up and tells us we can't go," he told the roan.

In the stalls around him, the horses whinnied and stamped, eager for their morning feeding. Sul frowned; the extra noise could bring his father down to the stable to investigate.

"All right, I'll feed you!" Sul said impatiently. He scampered up the ladder into the hayloft, tossed down hay through the overhang into the rack in the corral, and rattled back down to turn the dun and black loose. When they bolted past him into the corral, headed for the hayrack, he slammed open the lid of the feed box, scooped up a measure of corn apiece for his father's and Pete's horses and dumped the grain into their feed boxes. By then Saber was dancing impatiently himself.

Still wanting to clear out before his father appeared, Sul decided to clean the stalls after his ride. "Sorry, boy," he said to Saber, reaching down the blue's bridle, "no breakfast for you until we've had our run." He picked up his saddle but put it back down again. It would save time if he rode bareback.

He was standing in the roan's stall, buckling the throatlatch on the bridle, when the stable door opened. Fearing that it was his father, Sul stiffened and whirled to face this newcomer. He relaxed visibly when he saw that it was Hanse Mason who had come in.

If the sergeant noticed the boy's reaction, he did not show it. "You're up early," Mason said, closing the door behind him.

Sul started to explain about his extra chores, but the words died on his lips. It would sound like complaining, and Hanse didn't like bellyachers. "Saber needs a run," he said instead. "I thought I'd give him one before school."

Mason raised one eyebrow. "Before you've finished your chores?" he asked. The sergeant's eyes seemed to bore right through the boy and look down into the hurt at the core of his being.

Sul squirmed embarrassedly. He wanted to drop his eyes, but Mason held his gaze.

"You want to talk to me about it?" the sergeant asked.

The boy shook his head.

"Can you talk to your pa about it?" Mason went on.

"No!" Sul said suddenly. Leaving Saber tied, he stamped out of the stall and grabbed the pitchfork. "I'll do my chores before I go," he said gruffly.

He worked busily, cleaning out the stalls, while Mason gave his own horse hay and started his grooming. For about ten minutes the two of them went about their work in silence. Then Sul stopped and leaned on the pitchfork.

"Hanse, did you ever want more schooling?" he asked.

The sergeant paused in currying his sorrel's sides. "Many a time, young'un. Old Miz Mason taught me how to read an' write, but over the years there's been plenty times I've wished I'd known more. Could have been an officer, maybe, if I'd had more book learnin'."

"I do too," Sul said. "Lots more." He went back to work with the pitchfork.

Mason stood watching him for a few seconds before going on with his grooming. "I've got to finish my business early an' head back to the fort," the sergeant said, now busy with his brush. "But since your pa was tellin' me about the farm last night, I thought I'd ride out there for a look. You want to go with me?"

Sul grinned and set aside the pitchfork, his job of cleaning out the stalls finished. "Better even than breakfast," he said.

Mason reached for his own blanket and saddle. "It ain't often I get a chance to eat any cookin' as good as your ma's, so I don't want to miss breakfast. But we've got time for a ride if we make it pronto."

A few minutes later they were trotting down First Street bound for the family's farming acres a mile out of town. Happy to be on horseback and in the company of this good friend, Sul repeated his question about Napoleon. Mason paused thoughtfully before answering.

"He was Emperor as well as Supreme Commander, young'un," he said at last. "You have to remember that."

"But he left his soldiers to starve and freeze — and be cut to pieces by the Cossacks," Sul protested. "Even if he was Emperor, he should have stayed with his men."

"I ain't defendin' him," Mason said. "That's just how it was. Anyhow, you'd better learn now there are officers aplenty who think their rank makes 'em better than anybody else." They were out of the village now, and he spurred his horse into a canter.

Beside him, Sul heeled Saber into matching the pace. "What do you mean, Hanse?"

"That they figure they're due special privileges," the sergeant explained. "Maybe Bonaparte was the same way."

Sul considered this information. "Well," the boy said finally, "if I ever get to be an officer, I won't act like that."

Mason glanced sideways at him. "I thought we'd settled it that you're goin' to be a soldier — an' an officer — some day."

Horrified at the slip he had made, Sul turned his head away and did not answer. He did intend to be an officer some day, but right now he didn't want to talk about it. He didn't want Hanse — or anybody else, for that matter — to know he had overheard his father's talk of the night before.

For a short distance he rode in an uncomfortable silence, aware that Mason was studying him. Feeling himself blush under this close examination, he decided to divert the sergeant's attention. "I'll race you to that big oak tree," he said, pointing ahead down the lane which now had a rail fence.

Mason's harsh face relaxed. "You think you can outrun me?"

"I know I can. I told you Saber was fast." Sul patted the roan's neck. "He can jump, too, but I won't show you that today. Go on, Hanse, make a run for it — I'll even give you a head start."

"All right, young'un, let's see what that little horse can do." With a wave, the sergeant put spurs to his mount. The sorrel bounded into a gallop as Sul leaned forward over Saber's neck, loosened the reins, and kicked the blue into a run. With a thunder of hoofs the two riders sped down the lane, racing neck and neck. Then, as his stride lengthened, the smaller roan drew away from the larger horse until he was running at least two lengths ahead.

Sul cast a quick, triumphant grin over his shoulder at the sergeant and then bent closer over Saber's tossing mane, intent on winning this race. Ahead of them the lane ran through deep shade under several other trees before it passed the goal of their gallop. As Sul's horse entered the first patch of shade, a hog, which had chosen a muddy wallow in the road for a nap, bounded up with a squeal beneath the roan's feet.

Saber shied to the side in such an abrupt movement that it all but unseated Sul. For a second the boy thought he couldn't stay on, but somehow he kept his balance. By grabbing a handhold in Saber's mane and gripping hard with his knees, he was able to stay with the little horse until the roan crashed into the rail fence bordering the lane, lost his footing in the wet grass, and went down. Then and only then was the boy flung over the roan's head to land — hard — on his side a few feet away, the reins wrapped around one wrist.

Sul scrambled to his feet, bruised, muddied, and shaken as Mason rode up. By then Saber had regained his footing and was limping painfully on his left foreleg.

"Hanse, he's not hurt bad, is he?" Half crying, the boy untangled himself from the reins and stumbled forward to feel Saber's leg. Not finding any injury there, he then stood to run his hands over the roan's near shoulder. "If he's slipped a shoulder or something Pa will kill me — "

By then Mason had dismounted. He strode forward and, taking the boy by the shoulders, turned Sul to face him. "Your horse can wait!" he snapped. "An' as for your pa — he'd want to know if you're all right first. Are you hurt, young'un, other than that cut on your forehead? You took a bad spill."

"I — I don't think so." Sul wiped at the blood with a muddy sleeve and only succeeded in smearing his face worse. "I thought I was, though, when I first landed on my shoulder."

Mason felt the joint with practiced fingers. "Well," he said finally, "you ain't broke or dislocated it, if that's any comfort, but I reckon you'll be plenty stiff later. Let me patch you up so that you don't bleed all over your shirt, an' then we'll see what can be done for your horse."

"I've got a bandana. You look after Saber." Sul pulled a handkerchief from his pocket and dabbed at the cut with it. "The bleeding's almost stopped anyway," he said.

"Almost, but not quite," Mason retorted. "Between the mud an' the blood, your ma will have plenty to say when she sees you." He went to examine the roan while Sul watched anxiously.

"How badly is he lamed?" the boy asked when the sergeant at last straightened and stepped back.

"Not too bad — it's only a strain. You won't be able to ride him for a while, but I think we can get him back to town all right if we take it slow."

Sul relaxed at this news but sighed anyway. "Pa won't like it," he said. "There's going to be a racing meet Saturday, and I was supposed to ride Saber."

"You're lucky to be able to ride anythin' after that spill," Mason told him. "An' what would you have done if your horse had dragged you with your hand caught in the reins like that? Don't you have a knife so you could cut yourself free?"

Sul frowned. "Only an old barlow knife Pa gave me."

"I'll get you a knife, then. You're old enough to be trusted with a huntin' blade." Mason dug in his near saddlebag for his picket rope which he tied to Saber's bridle. "Let's get started back," he said, mounting and then putting out a hand to boost Sul up behind his saddle. "Chief here will carry double."

Sul nodded as he settled into place. "I can tell you right now Pa's not going to like what's happened," he said bleakly. He considered for a moment before shaking his head regretfully. "Or Ma either, for that matter," he added. "I just put this shirt on clean yesterday, and what's more, I've torn my britches."

Annie was just setting off to school when the sad little caval-cade paced into the dooryard of the cabin and halted. She put down her slate and books and ran back into the house, her pig-tails flying. "Ma, Ma," Sul heard her cry, "he's here! Hanse just brought him back home!"

Followed by all three of her daughters, Mrs. Ross hurried out of the cabin and down the steps. Sul slipped stiffly down from behind Mason's saddle and stood there, silent and ashamed, as his mother and two older sisters crowded around him.

"Son, you're hurt," Mrs. Ross began. She looked up at Mason, who by that time had also dismounted. "Hanse, what's hap-pened?"

"He took a spill, Miz Ross, but I don't think he's got anythin' wrong with him other than that cut an' some bruises. If I was you, though, I'd get him washed up to see if he's got any other cuts an' scrapes that need attention."

"Well, I thank you for bringing him home. Annie, child, run on to school before you're tardy. Tell Mr. Battle Sul may not be in class today. Mary, you and Margaret go put some water on to heat and get the washtub ready. Son, you're going to have to have a bath and then go to bed while we wash and dry your clothes."

Sul ducked his head. "You'll have to mend them, too, Ma," he said. He dropped his voice to a whisper. "I've ripped my britch-es," he confessed, blushing.

Mary gave a smothered laugh as she and Margaret went inside to carry out their mother's orders. Sul blushed even more, and this time Hanse wasn't any help.

"I'll see to his horse," the sergeant said, taking the reins of both animals and leading them toward the stable.

Sul was sitting in the kitchen after his bath, wrapped up in a quilt while waiting for his mother to bring him his nightshirt, when his father came storming in.

"I've just talked to Hanse, and sometimes I think he's got less gumption than you have," Shap Ross began. "The idea of encouraging you to race him — "

"Hanse didn't ask me to race, Pa — I asked him," Sul said wearily.

"Showing off again? Well, whichever way it was, I hope you're satisfied. You've lamed a valuable horse, torn your clothes, and bunged yourself up, and now your mother tells me you probably won't get to school today."

"I'm sorry, Pa. I won't show off again," the boy promised and meant it. Suddenly Sul was very tired. The cut on his forehead still stung from the soap Ma had used, his bruises were stiffening despite the warm bath, and he wanted nothing more at present than to go to his bed in the loft and sleep.

"You'd better not," his father said. "We can't afford many more days like today. Luckily Saber wasn't bad hurt."

"And neither was Sul," Mrs. Ross reminded her husband, coming in with the boy's nightshirt. "Hanse said it could have been a bad accident."

Shapley Ross snorted. "Boys Sul's age are like cats — whichever way you fling 'em, they'll land on their feet. Only thing is a cat's got better sense." He stomped to the door. "At least you've got your stray back," he called over his shoulder to his wife as he slammed out.

"Doesn't Pa care that I could have been hurt?" Sul asked. "Hanse said he would."

Mrs. Ross smiled and held out his nightshirt. "Right now your father is angry because you won't be able to race Saber on Saturday like he'd planned. But he's concerned — I heard him talking to Hanse about you."

Sul stood up to slip the garment on. He wanted to ask, "Then why doesn't he show me that he is?" Instead, he said, "If it's all right with you, Ma, I'm going to bed for a while."

"Of course, son," she agreed.

As he climbed the ladder into the loft, it seemed again to Sul that he had an anvil hanging around his neck.

RED ROVER

Raging hunger awakened Sul later. He sat up in bed, suddenly aware that he had not had anything to eat since supper the night before. Then he noticed someone had brought one of Pete's outgrown shirts and a pair of his britches up to the loft and left them on the bed for him to put on. As he dressed, rolling up the sleeves and britches legs, Sul wondered guiltily if he had ruined the other clothes beyond repair. "Pa will have plenty to say about it if I have," he thought resignedly.

Margaret was downstairs, sloshing milk in the churn to make butter, when Sul stiffly descended the ladder. Outside he could hear Mervin coughing and Annie fussing at Bob. Since Annie was home, that meant school was out. He wondered if he had missed working the ferry for the day, but before he could ask about that he needed to do something about his powerful hunger.

"Where's Ma?" he asked, glancing around. "I'm starved."

Margaret looked up from plunging the dasher up and down in the churn. "Over at the hotel. She said you could have some cornbread." His sister indicated a covered bowl on the table.

"And some buttermilk?" Sul asked hopefully.

"In a little while. But you can't have much — it won't be long until supper."

Sul nodded. So he had missed working the ferry that afternoon. Well, he thought, it couldn't be helped. If Pa had wanted him at the ferry, he would have wakened him. But as stiff and hungry as he was, he was glad his father had made other arrangements. Only for this afternoon, of course!

"Is Hanse still in town?" he asked, sitting down on a stool near Margaret so he could keep an eye on the butter making.

"No," his sister answered, "he left for Fort Graham this morning." As they talked, the dasher became harder to move up and down, signaling that the butter was forming. "This is about ready," his sister said at last, giving the dasher a couple of extra hard bangs. "Get yourself a mug so I can pour out."

Sul went for the bowl of cornbread instead. "Pour it over this," he said. "I love cornbread and buttermilk."

"You and Pa both." Margaret laughed, but she did as he asked.

Sul was finishing the last of the cornbread and buttermilk when his mother came in, followed by Annie, Mervin, and Bob. Still anxious about his clothes, he put his spoon and the bowl down and went to ask about them.

"They had to soak all afternoon, but we finally got them clean. They're on the line now. I sent Mary up with Pete's old clothes because I didn't think you would like to have to run around in your nightshirt while they dried like you used to do when you wore a wamus."

Sul blushed. "Like Bob?" he asked, looking at his youngest brother's bare legs beneath the long-tailed shirt the little boy wore. "No, thanks! I'd rather wear Pete's old clothes any day. Do I have time to water the horses before supper?"

"Just don't be too long," his mother said. "The stew is about done."

When Sul came back to the cabin after filling the horse

trough, he met his father carrying a hatchet and some other tools to the woodshed. Shap Ross greeted his son cheerfully. "There you are," the frontiersman said. "How are you feeling?"

Sul eyed his father warily. "Still a little stiff, Pa, but I'll be all right. You're in a good mood," he added.

"There's been a strong rise on the river, so the ferry traffic's picked up. And I talked to Mr. Patterson today — he's going to have to move a flock of sheep across the Brazos in the next couple of days. That'll bring in a good bit of cash."

Sul nodded. "Won't sheep jump off the ferry?"

His father smiled appreciatively. "Armistead and I spent all afternoon building barricades to pen them in so they can't. The sections are light enough so even you can set them up."

Sul relaxed at this news. "Does that mean you're going to let me keep operating the ferry?" he asked.

"As long as you continue to bring in the money." His father shook his head wonderingly. "Pete still can't figure out why you always make more than he does."

Sul started to tell him about the tips, but before he could do so, his father went on. "Here," Shap Ross said, holding out a hunting knife in a sheath attached to a leather belt, "Hanse and I got this for you. Just don't take it to school."

The boy's eyes sparkled. "I won't, Pa," he said, taking it from him and buckling it on. "And thank you."

"Thank Hanse when you see him again. He's the one who convinced me you needed a knife."

"Well, thanks for letting me have it," Sul replied. "Can I work the ferry all day tomorrow? It's Saturday."

His father frowned. "You might as well make yourself useful, since you won't be riding for me tomorrow."

Sul ducked his head guiltily. "I forgot about Saber," he admitted. "How is he?"

"Your horse should be all right in a couple of days, but it's for sure he can't be raced this meet."

"I know, and I'm sorry, Pa."

"Well, just don't let it happen again." Shap Ross finished putting the tools away and closed the woodshed door. "It's too bad you can't ride Sweetbriar, but she's due to foal soon and will have to stay out on the farm."

Sul nodded. Although he didn't want to be a farmer, he knew *that* much about horse raising. "We can race her later this summer."

"I'm counting on it," his father said. "Right now your duty's at the ferry. I'll have to show you how to set up the barricades in case Mr. Patterson decides to cross his flock tomorrow." He looked around as if judging the hour. "If we have time after supper, I'll show you tonight. What with the racing meet, there should be plenty of folks wanting to cross." Shapley Ross rubbed his hands gleefully as he started back to the cabin. "Too bad we can't get a whole passel of drovers wanting to cross their livestock over. At five cents a head, we could clean up."

The boy followed. "Yes, Pa," Sul agreed, but he wasn't thinking of what his father had just said. He was admiring the way his new knife hung on his belt.

As Sul left the cabin the next morning, bound for the ferry landing, he met Armistead, the family's servant. He led a team of oxen pulling a sledge fitted with a large keg.

"You off to the spring?" the boy asked, glad he didn't have Armistead's chore of filling the big keg at Waco Spring.

"Yessir, Marse Sul. Marse Shap expects me to take water around early. You ridin' for your pa today?"

"Not today," Sul told him. "Saber's lame, and you know Sweetbriar's due to foal soon. Unless Pa buys or trades for another horse, we don't have an entry."

"Bet your pa ain't happy about that."

"He'll get over it. Wish I could have ridden Lady Jane for Mr. Jonas today though." With a wave, Sul passed the sledge and hurried on down the hill, whistling as he went. On the whole, he was content with his work assignment for the day. "After all," he told himself, "I could have been given Armistead's job of delivering the water." Next to the speed and excitement of racing, he liked operating the ferry best.

About noon Shapley Ross came down to the ferry landing, bringing his son's dinner tied up in a bandana.

"Has the ferry traffic been heavy this morning?" he asked as Sul dug into the cornbread and cold bacon.

"Pretty heavy, Pa," Sul answered, his mouth full. "I've made five dollars."

"Let me have it." Shap Ross held out his hand.

Sul handed over the money. "Most of it's been farmers coming into town with their wagons or riders heading for the racing," he explained. "It should slow down once the races start."

"Has Mr. Patterson crossed yet?"

"Not yet, Pa, but I'll be on the lookout for him."

"See that you do," his father said and started back up the bluff.

Not long after Sul finished his meal, a rider on a sweating bay stallion trotted down the bluff, headed east. Brushing cornbread crumbs off his lap, Sul stood and went to greet this passenger. The horse looked familiar, but the man was a total stranger.

"How much to cross, sonny?" the man asked, dismounting and leading his stallion forward. He too was sweating.

"Twenty cents, sir," Sul said.

"All right, take me across." The man glanced nervously around. "Can you handle a horse?" he asked suddenly.

"Yes, sir," Sul told him. He would have added, "I do it for my pa all the time," but he was being careful not to brag.

The man nodded and shoved the bay's reins into Sul's hands. "Lead him on board," he directed. As Sul did so, the man walked up the hill a few yards to look back the way he had come. It seemed that he was listening for something.

Wondering, Sul led the bay to the center of the ferry. As he tied the stallion there he noticed an odd patch of white hair on the animal's near hock. Surely he had seen that same patch the last time he had ridden at Cameron against a bay stallion named Red Rover. Was it possible the horse had been stolen from his owner, Mr. Carrolton?

Sul decided to find out. "Red Rover," he called softly. He had the satisfaction of seeing the animal's ears flick and hearing the stallion give a low whinny in recognition. "So it is you," the boy said, giving the bay a comforting pat.

The rider came striding up, and Sul decided to test the fellow. "I didn't know Red Rover was for sale," he told the man. "Mr. Carrolton didn't mention it the last time we raced."

The man cursed under his breath and laid his hand on his pistol. "He changed his mind, kid. Now cast off. I've got to be in East Texas as soon as possible."

Sul glanced around, surer than ever that the stallion had been stolen. And the way this fellow was acting, pursuit must be only a short distance behind. If he could delay their crossing, those in pursuit would have a better chance of catching up with the man. He decided to try it.

"Hope you don't mind waiting for someone else," he said casually. "Pa likes me to save trips."

The stranger broke out into a greater sweat. "I'll pay you double," the man promised. "Only get me across."

Sul knew for sure then. "No," he began, "Pa said — "

"I'll pay you five dollars!" the man blurted out.

"That's not enough," Sul whined, trying how far he could push the horse thief. "Make it ten, mister!"

The stranger drew his pistol and leveled it at the boy. "Take me across now, you little brat! I told you I have to get to East Texas right away!"

"All right, all right!" Sul raised his hands and backed away. "I didn't know you were in such a hurry, mister!" Leaving the center of the ferry, the boy cast off and jerked the rope and pulley to start the ferry moving toward the far bank. He watched the man warily, but by then the stranger had turned his attention back to the way he had come.

As they got underway, two horsemen galloped down the Waco bank of the river. "Stop that ferry in the name of the law!" one of the men yelled after them, and Sul recognized the sheriff of Milam County. "That's a stolen horse!"

Whipping out his knife, Sul began cutting the rope pulling them to the far bank. It was almost cut through when the horsethief glanced back and realized what he was doing.

With another curse, the stranger made a grab at Sul, but the boy ducked out of his reach under the stallion's belly. As he emerged on the other side, Sul gave the bay a jab in the flank with his knife handle that caused the animal to start and kick. Keeping the kicking horse between himself and the horse thief, Sul backed until he felt the rail of the ferry behind him. As the tow rope parted, he turned and scrambled over the side where he clung to one of the mooring lines.

"Watch out," he yelled to the sheriff. "We're drifting back to that side."

"Don't worry, sonny," the lawman called back. "We won't let him get away!"

The rest was easy. His escape cut off, the horse thief surrendered quietly. Sul climbed back onto the ferry and joined the sheriff and his deputy with their prisoner near the landing.

"I'm glad you caught him," the boy said eagerly, ignoring the prisoner's hateful glare. "I didn't think Mr. Carrolton had sold Red Rover. He wouldn't the last time Pa asked him."

The sheriff nodded. "You're Captain Ross' son, ain't you?"

Sul grinned up at him. "Yes, sir."

"I thought I recognized you. So you knew Red Rover, hey, and cut the rope so we could catch the man who stole him?"

"Oh, yes, sir," Sul said.

"Well, I'm proud of you, boy, and that's a fact."

Sul beamed. "That should prove to Pa that I have more in me than just being a farmer," he told himself. To the sheriff he said, "Could you tell my pa how I helped you? He'd like to know. And can you help me get the rope strung back across?"

"Sorry, sonny, but we've got to get back." The sheriff tightened his reins as if about to start.

Sul stepped forward and laid his hand on the lawman's bridle. "Please, sir. It'll save me a hiding."

The lawman grinned broadly. "Can't do that — we don't have time. Tell you what, though — I'll speak to your pa on our way out of town. Where can I find him?"

That was what Sul wanted to hear. "Pa usually hangs out at the hotel or Barnard's Store, but today he's probably at the racing meet on Second Street. Most other folks will be."

"We'll find him," the sheriff promised.

Hands on hips, Sul watched the three horsemen climb the bluff and ride over the crest. Then he turned and did a gleeful war dance on the ferry landing. "Top that, Mr. West Point Pete!" he hollered happily, as if his brother were right there to hear his crow of victory. "You've never helped catch a horse thief." Grinning broadly, Sul turned his attention back to the task of making repairs.

TO THE WOODSHED

Washed in a warm inner glow of happiness, Sul surveyed his problem. The first thing, he decided, was to get the ferry back into operation again. Once the sheriff talked to Pa, his father would probably come down to the landing to congratulate him on his exploit. Knowing Pa, it would mean so much more if he could present his father with an accomplished fact and the ferry working once more.

Leaning over the side of the ferry, Sul grasped the now slack rope and began to pull it hand over hand back on board. As the last of it came out of the water and lay in wet coils on the deck, he realized that the propelling rope had slipped free of the pulley fastened at the other landing.

"Drat!" he said. "It'll have to be restrung!" Squatting over the rope, the boy puzzled what he should do next. Although he understood how the ferry worked, he had been in school the day the rope had been strung from bank to bank, and he didn't know exactly how it had been done. And, he wondered, holding the cut end of the rope in one hand, could he even do it by himself? "I'll probably need a skiff to take the rope back over to the other side," he told himself.

Hoofbeats coming down the hill from the village caused him to start guiltily, and he glanced up to see Mr. Patterson riding toward the landing. "Oh, no," Sul groaned. "He would show up now." Dropping the rope, he jumped up and went to meet the newcomer as the man drew rein.

"Hi, Mr. Patterson," the boy said nervously. "Are your sheep on the way?"

"Lot of good it will do me if they are," the farmer answered angrily, looking around at the disabled ferry. "Your pa said you'd be able to take us across, but I see now he was mistaken. Just wait until I tell him the ferry's out of commission — " He reined his horse around.

"Wait — please!" Sul ran after him, but the man had already given his mount a cut with the reins and was cantering back up the hill.

"Pa's not going to like this — even if I did help catch a horse thief," Sul told himself, slowing to a stop. His shoulders sagging dejectedly, the boy turned back to the ferry landing where he plumped himself down on the keg he used as a seat.

He knew he was in trouble sometime later when he saw his father come boiling down the hill.

"I should have known you were too young and reckless to run this operation!" Shapley Ross yelled as soon as he was in earshot. "What have you done now? You've cost us plenty in fares!"

"Didn't the sheriff tell you?" Sul asked when his father came stamping up to him. "He said he was going to explain what happened."

"What sheriff?" Shap Ross roared.

Watching an ominous muscle twitch in his father's jaw, Sul faltered. "The — the sheriff of Milam County," he stammered.

"What are you talking about?" his father shouted. "What does the sheriff of Milam County have to do with your stupidity in putting the ferry out of service just when Mr. Patterson was ready to cross? What did you do — skylark around and get the rope broken?"

Sul winced. "Pa, I — "

Without waiting for a further explanation, Shapley Ross pushed past his son and hopped on board the ferry. He stooped over the rope, and fishing up the cut end, thrust it into Sul's face. "This rope has been cut!" he bellowed.

Sul blinked and stepped back. "Pa, I helped the sheriff catch a horse thief," he said. "I was taking the man across when the sheriff and one of his deputies rode up. I cut the rope so we'd drift back over here."

Shap Ross snorted. "A likely story. Don't lie to me, Sul!"

"Pa, I'm not lying," Sul protested. "Ask the sheriff! He promised he would speak to you."

"Well, he didn't! And I don't think he was ever here." Shap Ross began unfastening his belt. "I don't know where you got that cock-and-bull story about a horse thief," he said, "but I told you before what would happen if you skylarked around and didn't do your job properly. Walk ahead of me to the woodshed."

Sul started to protest further, but then he decided there was no use in doing so, as angry as his father was. Squaring his shoulders and walking as straight as an Indian, he started up the hill to the woodshed and the hiding that awaited him there.

The licking which followed was a sound one. Despite the thoroughness of the thrashing, Sul did not cry, and after the hiding was over, he stood before his father, his face pale and drawn but free from tears.

"Admit you've lied," Shap Ross ordered.

Sul shook his head even though he knew it would make his father even angrier.

"Admit you've lied, or you won't operate the ferry again," the elder Ross yelled.

"Then I won't operate the ferry again," Sul replied coldly. He put up his chin. "Because whatever you say, Pa, I didn't lie."

"All boys lie to save their hides," his father said.

"I didn't," Sul answered proudly. He didn't resist, even when his father grabbed him by the collar and licked him again.

Later, when he had been sent to bed without any supper as an additional punishment, Sul lay on his stomach on his bed in the loft. The welts raised on his backside by his father's belt were subsiding, although they still burned. But nothing could ease the pain in his heart, the dull ache he felt from being considered not only untrustworthy but a liar. His father was frequently unfair, but today his injustice galled Sul more than ever before. And to be thought a liar on top of the injustice was almost more than the boy could bear.

Gradually he became aware of heated voices downstairs. Usually his mother didn't interfere in her husband's discipline of their sons, but today, if Sul was hearing properly, she was protesting strongly.

"You could at least have asked around if anyone saw the sheriff in town today before you accused Sul of lying," Mrs. Ross told her husband.

"Boys will always lie to save their hides," her husband repeated.

"But you could go make sure," his wife answered.

"Anything for peace in the family!" Shap Ross slammed out of the cabin.

In the silence which followed, Sul at last fell asleep. He awakened much later to find Pete crawling into bed.

"Sul!" his brother whispered loudly.

The boy decided to ignore him and pretend to be asleep. His eyes closed, he lay absolutely still.

"Don't play possum with me," Pete went on. "I know you're awake."

Sul rolled over then to confront his brother. "What is it to you?" he demanded in a fierce whisper, raising himself stiffly into a sitting position.

"Why didn't you admit to Pa that you'd lied?" Pete asked.

"Because I didn't, that's why!" Sul snapped.

"That's not what Pa is saying," Pete went on. "He asked around town and found the sheriff of Milam County had been here, but that the sheriff was telling folks he caught that horse thief on the ferry landing."

"Then the sheriff's a liar," Sul snarled. Flopping back down, he turned over on his side so that his back was to his brother.

But Pete wasn't finished. "Pa's going to put you to work hauling water," he said. And then, as if to rub it in, the oldest Ross son added, "That's all he says you're fit for right now."

Sul's only open answer was another snarl. Inside, though, he was seething. "Why couldn't Pa have told me about the water-hauling job himself rather than leaving it up to Pete?" he asked himself hotly. And the disgrace of switching jobs — wasn't it enough that Pa had taken the ferry operation away from him? Right now he hated his father and Pete — and the sheriff of Milam County. "When I grow up," he vowed furiously to himself, "I'm not going to accuse *my* sons falsely or lie to a child — ever." As he made this vow, tears stung his eyes, but Sul fought them back. "Soldiers don't cry," he told himself fiercely.

Two days later, Sul was yoking the oxen to the water barrel sledge when Armistead hurried up.

"Mighty fine news, Marse Sul," the family servant said, grinning broadly. "Old Miz Oakes' Jake was down by the river fishin' the other day when you helped the sheriff catch that horse thief. He saw an' heard the whole thing, chile."

Sul glanced up from fastening the off yoke. "Have you told Pa?" he asked eagerly.

"Not yet, but I'm a gettin' ready to soon as I sees him. The idea of that sheriff lyin' like that — "

Sul felt as if a hundred-pound sack of corn had been lifted from his shoulders. Gleefully, he turned and gave Armistead a hug. "Thanks, Armistead. That's the best news I've had since Hanse was here."

"Chile, I only wished I'd talked to Jake sooner. Maybe you'd been saved that hidin'."

Sul shrugged. Suddenly it didn't matter so much. "Pa might have licked me anyway for putting the ferry out of service," he admitted, trying to be fair. "At least now he'll know I didn't lie — that's the main thing."

"That's mighty important," Armistead agreed. He waved as he walked off. "I'm goin' to look for your pa right now," he said.

Grinning, Sul returned the wave. As he went about filling the keg and delivering the water to his father's customers that day, he considered just how he should act when his father came to him to apologize. At last he decided the big-hearted approach would be best. "That's all right, Pa," he would say with a generous smile, "we all make mistakes." Then his father would praise him for his courage and quick thinking in capturing the horsethief. Maybe Pa would even ask if there was something he could do to make up for the misunderstanding. "If he does," Sul told himself, "I'll tell him I don't want to be a farmer — that I want a chance to go to West Point, just like Pete."

Sul could hardly wait to get home that evening. Throughout the afternoon he had looked for his father to come to him as he made the rounds with the water deliveries, but Shap Ross had not done so. Now the boy was expecting his father to apologize at supper, but that meal passed without a word spoken to him. Wondering, Sul watched his father closely. Shapley Ross seemed the same as usual, and the boy began to panic. Soon the evening would pass and then it would be time for bed. Had Armistead forgotten to speak to his father, or had he too betrayed Sul's trust?

Heartsick, Sul went about his evening chores. He was shutting the horses up for the night when Armistead slipped into the stable. "Did you talk to Pa?" the boy asked sharply.

Tears filled the man's eyes. "Marse Sul, I done talked to your pa, an' he believed me, but I don't reckon he's goin' to apologize. I reckon he's too ashamed to admit he made a mistake."

"He's ashamed?" Sul yelled. "What about me? Doesn't he realize he's shamed me by accusing me of something I never did?"

Armistead nodded vigorously. "I done told him that, chile, but he ain't listenin'. You knows Marse Shap when he gets bullheaded — ain't nobody but maybe your ma an' Marse Hanse can talk him around an' sometimes even they can't do it."

Sul turned and kicked the empty feed bucket savagely. It flew across the stable with a clatter and bounced off the wall of one of the stalls, causing his father's horse to shy the length of its tether. "I hate Pa," he said bitterly.

WHAT WOULD NAPOLEON DO?

S witch in hand, Sul slouched along beside the oxen pulling the water sledge, glumly thinking over the conversation he had that morning with Armistead. "It's been over two weeks since Pa hided me for the ferry incident, and he still hasn't admitted he made a mistake," Sul had protested heatedly. "Isn't he ever going to say anything?"

"Chile, I doubt your pa'll ever apologize for that hidin' he give you," Armistead had answered. "Best not expect it. Just pick up from here an' go on."

"If it had been Pete I bet he would have — " Sul began, but he broke off when he saw Armistead shake his head.

"Not even for Marse Pete. Marse Shap ain't the apologizin' kind, especially not to his sons. He wants you all to grow up to be strong men, an' he's scared you all won't if he lets up on discipline. Why you so set on him apologizin' anyways?" the servant went on. "He done give you a hidin' before when we all knowed he was wrong. Marse Pete too. Is it because you ain't gettin' to work the ferry no more?"

"That's part of it," Sul agreed. "But I've got to prove to Pa that I can be a soldier, Armistead, I've just got to! I've got to do something that'll cause Pa to sit up and take notice. But what can it be?"

"Marse Sul, I don't know! But you an' Marse Pete is both plenty smart. You'll come up with somethin'."

Still considering the question as he made his rounds, Sul turned the ox team down a side street. As he approached the better section of town, he spotted three older boys lounging around in the front yard of one of the village's wealthier citizens. Sul pulled himself up straight, trying to put as much dignity as possible into his appearance but nevertheless feeling ashamed as the oxen plodded down the street past the group.

He had hoped to escape the trio's notice, but he was to have no such luck. "Look at Sul Ross," one of the boys crowed, pointing at him. "He's doing nigger work!"

"Yeah, Sul," called another. "What's the matter? Did the paterollers pick up Armistead, and you have to do his job?"

"Naw," said the third, snickering. "Sul's got ferry problems, haven't you, Sul?"

His ears burning, Sul stiffened himself into an even prouder stance and walked quietly by. "I'm not afraid of you," he said under his breath, "but I've got a job to do. Just wait 'til I'm not on duty."

"Hey!" hollered the first boy, "I'm talking to you!" Out of the corner of his eye Sul saw him stoop and then throw something. The boy ducked, but the stone still struck him in the head. The blow staggered Sul, knocking him to one knee, but he immediately leaped back to his feet, holding one hand to his scalp as blood ran down his cheek.

"I'll get you for that, Davy Briscoe!" he yelled at the rock thrower but found he was speaking to empty air. All three of his tormenters had fled as soon as they realized that the stone had drawn blood.

"Just wait until I don't have this ox team to control — I'll show you," Sul vowed. He fished in his pocket for his bandana and held it to the place as he urged his team on. He was still holding the bandana there when Pete came trotting by on his dun, bound home from his special tutoring.

Pete jerked his horse to a halt beside his brother. "What happened?" he asked sharply. "You've got blood all down your face — and on your shirt."

"Someone chunked a rock at me," Sul said. His tone was grim.

Pete was out of his saddle instantly. "Let me see," he ordered.

Reluctantly, Sul pulled the bandana away so that his brother could examine the place.

"That's deep," Pete said finally. "No wonder you bled like a stuck pig. Who did it?"

"Davy Briscoe."

Pete clenched his fists. "That skunk — just because his pa's got more money than anyone else in Waco, he thinks he can — " The older boy broke off and put a comforting hand on Sul's arm. "You want me to go thrash him for you?"

"In your good clothes?" Sul asked bitterly, pulling away from him. "I wouldn't want you to get a hiding because of me."

Pete grabbed him by the shoulders and shook him. "Pa wouldn't care, not if I was standing up for my brother when he needed it! That's what big brothers are for! Now do you want me to whip Davy for you?"

Sul's bitterness melted, and he grinned. "No, I want to do it myself."

"He's bigger than you are," Pete reminded him.

Sul waved this concern away. "I'm not afraid of Davy."

Pete eyed him closely. "No," he admitted finally after studying his brother's determined expression, "I don't guess you are." It was his turn to grin. "In fact, if I were Davy, I'd be afraid of you!"

Sul returned his brother's smile. "If you would, Pete, help me wash the blood off before I go home to Ma. If I've bled as much as you say, I don't want to scare her."

"It would take a whole lot more than that blood to frighten Ma," Pete answered stoutly, "but Mary and Annie would squeal for sure if they saw you. Margaret's got better sense, though. Have you got anything left in the keg?"

"A couple of bucketfuls."

"Well, this is one time when I don't think Pa will miss the money," Pete said.

"If it is, it'll be the first time," Sul answered, and they both laughed.

That evening, as the boys lay companionably in bed just before sleep, Pete asked, "Have you figured out how to pay Davy Briscoe back yet?"

In the darkness of the loft, Sul smiled to himself before answering. "Don't worry — I'm thinking. I'll come up with a strategy — just you wait and see." In his own mind, he added to himself, "And I'll show you, too, Pa — I'll show you I can plan and carry out a campaign."

Three nights later, the boys were in the kitchen getting ready for their Saturday baths in the washtub when Sul paused in his undressing and grinned impishly at his brother. "I've been reading more about Bonaparte," he said, "and I've got an idea for dealing with Davy Briscoe. I'll need you to do some scouting for me, though."

Pete returned the grin. "Glad to. What do you need to know?"

Sul shed the last of his clothes and stepped into the tub. "See if you can find out the way he goes to school," he said, taking up the washrag and soap. "I'd do it myself, but I don't want to give my plans away."

His brother grinned again and gave him a mock salute. "Yes, sir, *General* Ross!" he teased. Leaning over Sul, Pete took the soap and washrag from his brother's hand. "Duck down and get yourself wet," he directed. "I'll scrub your back if you'll scrub mine."

Monday evening when the boys met at supper, Pete gave his brother a secret wink. "I had Joe Thompson find out for me," he told Sul later. "Davy always takes the short cut through the Widow Temple's woods. The only thing is, Percy Eubanks usually walks with him."

Sul snorted. "That sissy? He's got a big mouth but not much fight. Besides, being outnumbered never bothered Bonaparte."

Pete laughed. "Still, he met his Waterloo. Just be sure you don't do the same."

"If I do, I'll go down fighting," Sul promised.

The next morning Sul got up even earlier than usual, rushed through his chores, and was racing to school long before Pete and Annie started that direction themselves.

Reaching the schoolhouse well ahead of any of his schoolmates, Sul hid his books in the hollow of a nearby oak tree and hurried back the way he had come. Before he reached the main part of the village, however, he turned off the road which led back to the Ross cabin and looked for a hiding place in the grove of trees known as the Widow Temple's woods.

"Just the thing," Sul said to himself, spotting a low branch hanging over the path. Nimble as a squirrel, he climbed the tree and took his seat on the branch. Then all he had to do was wait.

Presently Davy Briscoe and his friend Percy came strolling along the path, talking and laughing. Grinning to himself, Sul waited until the pair had passed under his hiding place. Then, with a Comanche yell, he dropped to the path behind them.

Percy turned and saw the avenging fury hurtling toward them. "Davy, run!" he yelled, bolting past Sul back down the path.

"Run if you want to, coward!" Sul hollered over his shoulder. "I don't care about you, anyway!" Concentrating all his will on thrashing his enemy, he waded into Davy.

"Ow, Sul! No! Stop!" yelled his victim as the flailing fists whirled around him, landing blows right and left, now on his nose, next on his chin.

"Holler enough!" Sul ordered fiercely, knocking his opponent to the ground and rolling him there. "Surrender or I'll knock the stuffing out of you."

The bigger boy began to cry. "I give up," he whimpered.

"Say you're sorry you threw that rock," Sul demanded.

"Sorry," Davy repeated ungraciously.

Sul sat back then so that his foe could sit up. For a moment Davy glared at his conqueror; then he asked, "Will you help me up so I can shake hands?"

"Sure," Sul said. He helped the older boy to his feet, and then trustingly put out his hand for the handshake which would signal the end of the fight. Instead, he received a facer which knocked him flat.

Sul jumped to his feet in time to see Davy take to his heels, arms and legs pumping like the rocker arms of a Mississippi steamboat as he ran. "Come back here, you coward!" he yelled, bounding after the other boy. "I'll pound you every day for a week because of that!" The older boy's only answer was to put on an extra burst of speed which soon outdistanced his pursuer.

Fists clenched, Sul panted to a stop and watched the object of his pursuit swing around the corner of Mrs. Oakes' yard fence and make a dash for home and safety. He stood there, breathing deeply to get air back into his lungs, and then the humor of the incident struck him. For a few minutes laughter so doubled him up that he had to cling to the fence to stay upright.

"Sul, is everything all right?" asked a timid voice behind him. "I heard a ruckus and saw Davy Briscoe run past. You aren't hurt, are you?"

Still chuckling, Sul turned to face Charley Oakes who had come up on the other side of the fence. The other boy was small and thin. In many ways he reminded Sul of Mervin. "I'm fine, Charley," he said and then grinned at his friend. "Davy Briscoe shouldn't be feeling too smart right now, though — I pounded him good."

Charley's pale face lit up, and he clapped his thin hands. "I'm glad you did," he said feelingly. "I've wanted to for a long time. He picks on me because I'm little."

Sul dusted his hands energetically. "Maybe he'll leave us both alone after this. Are you feeling better? We've missed you at school."

"Some, but I'm not going back to school — at least not now," Charley told him. "Next week Ma's taking me out to Liz's place at Fort Graham so that she can teach me. Liz was a schoolmistress back in Tennessee before she married Mr. Barton."

Sul nodded. "I remember your mother saying something about it when they stayed with you last year." Behind him he could hear the distant ringing of the school bell. If he didn't hurry, he'd be tardy. "Sorry, but I've got to go, Charley. If you see Hanse while you're staying with your sister, tell him hello for me."

"I will," his friend promised. "I only wish I could have seen you pound Davy Briscoe."

"I wish Pa could have seen me," Sul called over his shoulder as he headed back to the schoolhouse.

When school was out at noon, Pete rejoined him for the walk home. "What happened?" his brother asked as they started off, Annie walking a few steps behind to talk to a school friend. "I noticed Davy was late getting to school this morning."

Sul grinned. "I divided his force and rolled up his right — just like Napoleon!"

"Any trouble?"

"Not until he wanted to shake hands. Then he smacked me one and ran." Sul chuckled again at the memory. "It was funny, Pete," he said when he saw his brother frown. "He won't trick me again."

"I still say he's a skunk — " Pete began, but he broke off when Annie came trotting up to walk between her brothers.

"What's funny, Sul?" their sister asked, her eyes big. "And who's a skunk, Pete?"

"Nobody who concerns you," Pete said. "It's just man talk between Sul and me."

Annie poked her nose up in the air. "Man talk, huh! I think

Sul's been fighting again, and you know how Ma feels about that." She hurried ahead of her brothers. "Just wait till I tell her," she called over one shoulder.

"Annie, don't worry Ma — " Sul started after her, but Pete grabbed his sleeve and held him back.

He shook his head at his brother. "Leave her alone, Sul. Ten to one she'll forget about it before she gets home. Besides, we answer to Pa, not Ma, for something like fighting. Pa understands that a man's got to fight sometimes."

But this, it seemed, was not to be one of those times. When the boys reached the cabin, Sul found their father on the gallery waiting for them, and even at a distance he could tell that Shapley Ross was hopping mad.

"Go inside!" Shap Ross told Pete roughly when they walked up. "My business is with your brawling buccaneer of a brother!"

"Pa, I — " Pete started to say something, but their father cut him off short.

"Inside!" Shap Ross bellowed.

Sul saw Pete give him a helpless look, and then he went into the cabin as ordered. Sul was left facing their father alone.

"Did you or did you not ambush and thrash Davy Briscoe and Percy Eubanks?" Shap Ross demanded.

Sul could tell his father was almost beside himself with anger. He sighed. There was no use trying to explain things to Pa when he was that mad, but he decided to try anyway. "Ambush them both, yes," he answered, putting up his chin resolutely. "Thrash them both, no. Percy ran. But I whaled the tar out of Davy. He hit me with a rock when I was delivering water the other day."

But Shapley Ross wasn't listening. "Two of the leading men of Waco — some of our best customers — and you treat their sons like white trash!" He grabbed Sul by the collar and pulled off his belt. "To the woodshed!" he ordered.

RUNAWAY

"Sul?" Pete called softly, climbing the ladder into their sleeping loft later that afternoon. "Hey, Sul. Are you awake?"

"Go away," Sul answered, his voice muffled by his pillow. "I don't want to talk to you." He lay on his side with his face toward the wall.

Pete ignored his plea. "I talked to Pa. Percy Eubanks told his pa you pulled a knife on him and Davy."

"Percy didn't stick around to see what I did," Sul retorted, still without turning to face Pete. "He always was a liar."

"I told Pa that too," Pete said. "And I let him know that you left your knife up here when you went to school, because I saw it after you left. Listen, Sul, he's sorry he licked you without really listening to your side of the story."

"Then tell him to come tell me so himself!" Sul snapped. "That's twice lately Pa's hided me for something I didn't do."

There was an uncomfortable silence on Pete's part, and Sul turned painfully over on one elbow to face his brother. "He's not coming this time, either, is he?" he asked.

Pete nodded miserably. "I'm sorry, Sul. You know Pa. He — "

Sul turned back on his other side so that he was facing the wall again. "Oh, go away!" he shouted over his shoulder at Pete. "I said in the first place I didn't want to talk to you. And I don't want to talk to Pa, or Ma, or anybody else!" he added savagely. "Leave me alone!"

Pete spoke again. "Try to be a little more understanding, Sul. Sweetbriar died today giving birth to her foal, and then the foal died too, so Pa's out all that money he paid for her. That was one of the reasons he came down on you so hard. Besides, right now Pa isn't even here. He left on the stage for Houston. There's going to be a big racing meet down there, and he hopes to buy a new mare."

Sul faced his brother again. "I'm sorry about Sweetbriar," he said, "but Pa can be a little more understanding with me, too. Now go away! I don't want to live here any more — I want to go live with Uncle Isaac!"

"Pa wouldn't let you do that," Pete told him.

"Then I'll go to Hanse at Fort Graham," Sul said.

"You're needed here, and he'd send you back. You know how he feels about a man doing his duty."

Reluctantly, Sul agreed, and Pete went on. "Face it, Sul, you'll have to stay here with us." He smiled encouragingly at his brother. "Pa was just on a rampage earlier. It'll be all right when he gets back from Houston — you'll see."

"That's easy for you to say," Sul retorted. "Pa's got your future planned, and you like it. Well, I don't like what he's got planned for me. I want to be a soldier, not a farmer. If I went to live with Uncle Isaac maybe he could get me an appoint — "

"Forget it," Pete said, starting back down the ladder. "Pa would never allow you to go to Missouri. And if you run away, he'll go after you and bring you back. So don't try it, Sul."

Fighting back the tears he felt for Sweetbriar, her foal, and himself, Sul lay staring at the loft roof and considering the undeniable truth of this statement. "I still wish I could go live with Uncle Isaac," he repeated stubbornly.

The ladder creaked as Pete came back into the loft. "I almost forgot — Abel Corrigan can't work the ferry tomorrow after school, so Pa says you're to do it for him. Then you're to go back to hauling water."

"So Pa's decided I am fit to work the ferry? Thanks a lot!"

Pete grinned. "He doesn't know how you manage it, but you always make more than the rest of us."

"Well, that's too bad because I'm not going to do it!" Sul said. "Pa doesn't intend to give me any more schooling after this year, so I don't intend to make him any more money!"

"Pa'll hide you some more," Pete warned.

"He'll have to get back from Houston first," Sul answered.

Pete sighed. "You'd get along better with Pa if you'd only bend more."

"Like you?" Sul shook his head. "Pa's a tyrant, Pete. You'd see that if you weren't his favorite."

Pete sighed again and started back down the ladder. "I've got to go to tutoring," he said.

"So you can go to West Point while I have to stay at home on the farm!" Sul shouted after him. Suddenly his future stretched before him as a dreary round of hauling water, misunderstandings, and hidings, only briefly varied by horse racing and ferry operating, and finally, when he was old enough, the boring life of a farmer. And over all loomed the formidable shadow of his father, belt in hand.

"No, Pa! No!" Sul cried, pounding his pillow furiously. "I won't stay and let you make me into a farmer! I won't! I'll run away and go live with Chief José María and his Indians first! Just see if I don't!"

For a few moments after making this vow, Sul lay still, considering the possibility of running away. "Pa won't be back for a week at least, and I can be long gone by then," he said to himself. "Hanse said José María was honorable. If I tell the chief Pa would only beat me again if he sent me home, surely he'll let me stay."

Another few minutes passed while Sul thought of how pleasant life would be with Chief José María and his Anadarkos and away from his father and his belt. Downstairs he could hear his mother and Mary talking about what they were going to cook for supper. Mervin coughed loudly. He was sick again and had been put to bed in the kitchen.

Sul's conscience bothered him when he thought about leaving his mother, especially with Mervin sick, but the boy quickly brushed those misgivings aside. "I've got to prove myself to Pa," he said, rolling over. "I've just got to. If I go live with the Anadarkos for awhile, that should show him I'm cut out to be more than just a farmer."

Then the cabin door banged. "Ma, Ma!" Annie said breathlessly, coming inside, "Katie Johnson says their new baby's on the way and her mother needs your help!"

"This early?" Mrs. Ross said. "Tell Katie I'll be right there. Mary, you come help me with the Johnson children. Annie, you keep an eye on Bob until Margaret gets back. She's sewing on a dress at Millie's. Mervin will be all right until then."

"Yes, Ma," Annie answered, going back outside. She was followed almost immediately by Mrs. Ross and Mary. Soon all was quiet downstairs.

His mind racing, Sul hopped out of bed and pulled on his socks and boots. From a small trunk he took the sky blue silk neckerchief Mary's suitor, George Barnard, had recently given him and tied it around his neck. "It'll be just the thing to protect my nose and mouth from dust out on the plains," he told himself. Then, buckling on the belt with his hunting knife, he went down the ladder into the kitchen. There he collected his rifle, powder horn, and shot pouch from the gunrack and took the case containing his Baby Dragoon Colt down from the shelf.

Behind him Mervin sighed and turned in his sleep. Sul started guiltily and froze, but his younger brother did not wake up.
Relieved, Sul went on with his packing.

In one burlap sack he stowed the Colt, some extra lead for
bullets, and a flint and steel; in another he placed the biscuits
left over from breakfast, some salt in a twist of paper, and three
cooked sweet potatoes. His next meal taken care of, Sul headed
for the door. As he halted to put on his hat, the door opened and
Annie bounced in, leading Bob. Her mouth fell open when she
saw her brother standing there with his arms loaded.

"Where are you going?" she gasped.

"I'm running away," Sul answered.

"I'll tell Ma!"

"Tell her, then! But you won't stop me." He hefted his load.

Annie began crying. "What about Ma?" she sobbed. Not to be
outdone, Bob started to howl himself. That woke Mervin up,
and he too began to cry.

"I don't want to hurt Ma, but I can't live here with Pa any
longer," Sul said. "She'll be all right — she has the rest of you."
He pushed past his sister and brother and ran for the stable without looking back.

Saber whinnied a low "wuh-huh-huh" of greeting as the boy
entered. "I know you're eager for a run," Sul told the roan as he
started his saddling, "but it'll have to wait. First I've got to make
sure we aren't followed."

Minutes later he led the horse from the stable and halted outside to swing into the saddle. No one was in sight as he trotted
around the corner of the family cabin and headed Saber downhill to the ferry landing.

"Abel, can you take me across right away?" Sul asked when he
rode up to the moored ferry.

The lanky Irishman got to his feet. "Sure thing, Mister Sul."
As the ferry got under way, Corrigan eyed the boy's rifle and
powder horn. "You going hunting?"

"You could say that," Sul answered truthfully, knowing he would have to hunt to live once his supplies ran out. "How far is it to Clarksville?"

Abel scratched his head. "About a hundred and fifty miles — I think. Never been myself. You planning to go there?"

"Someday," Sul replied.

On the east side of the Brazos he remounted Saber and made a big show of setting off at a fast lope on the road leading to Dallas and northeast Texas. Once out of sight of the ferry, however, he turned off the road and circled back through a wooded area north of the landing.

"Wait here, boy," he said, tying Saber well back in the trees. "I've got to watch for Pete." Taking one of the sweet potatoes from his food sack, Sul crept forward through the cover to a place where he could watch the ferry.

He did not have long to wait. Before he could finish eating the sweet potato, he spotted a familiar figure on a dun horse racing down the bluff bound for the ferry.

Sul crouched down behind a bush and strained his ears to hear what Pete was saying. Even at this distance the eldest Ross son's voice carried angrily over the water.

"Have you seen Sul?" Pete demanded of Abel.

"I crossed him less than an hour ago," the ferryman said.

"Then take me over after him," Pete ordered, leading his horse on board. Once the ferry was in motion, he went on. "Do you know where he's going? The little sneak's run away."

"Well, he didn't rightly say," Corrigan replied, "but he did ask me how far it was to Clarksville."

"He's headed for Missouri, then," Pete said through gritted teeth.

"When he left here, he was on the road to Dallas," Corrigan said. "I kind of wondered about it at the time. I hope you catch him before he gets himself in trouble."

"He's already in trouble," Pete raged, remounting as the ferry glided into the other landing. "Just wait until I get my hands on him — he won't be able to sit down for a week."

Listening to this exchange, Sul grinned. He watched Pete jump his dun off the boat as soon as the ferry docked and gallop off. Then he ran to get Saber.

"Come on, boy," he told the roan, untying his reins. "We'll be back across the river and well on our way west before Pete figures out that I've tricked him." He chuckled. "Abel's head really will spin when we ride up and I ask him for passage back."

As Sul had guessed, Abel Corrigan gaped at him when he returned to the landing. "Your brother's looking for you," the Irishman said, "and he's mad. He thinks you've run away."

Sul grinned. "Just take me back across, will you, Abel? Pete's just like Pa — he always gets mad when he thinks he's been out-smarted."

"And who's outsmarting him — you?" Corrigan asked.

"I hope so," Sul replied.

Back on the Waco side, Sul turned Saber's head toward the northwest. First he skirted the northern and then the western-most of the village's houses. Finally he chose lanes which would lead him south to the farm.

"I'm taking a chance, boy, by letting us be seen this side of the river," he told Saber, "but we'll soon be on our way. First, though, I want to grab that deerskin I have drying on the barn door and get you a bag of corn from the feed room."

No one was around when Sul dismounted at the door of the barn some time later. For an instant he thought of Sweetbriar and her foal, wondering where the dead horses were, but then he shook off the sadness that he felt. "We'll hide here for awhile," he told the horse, resolutely leading him inside. "Then we'll pull stakes for the trading post on the Bosque." Working quickly, the boy tied Saber in one of the stalls and shook down some hay into the manger. As the blue roan began eating, Sul shoved several measures of corn into an empty sack and tied it to his saddle. He had just jerked the deerskin down from the half open door and was beginning to roll it up when the rattle of a wagon from the lane made him look that way.

"Uh-oh, Armistead and Jake," Sul said, recognizing the pair on the wagon box as the two-mule vehicle rolled into the barnyard. "Come on, Saber, we can't let them catch us here." Throwing the deerskin across his saddle, the boy led his horse to the door and peered out as the wagon halted a few feet away.

"Let's hurry up an' bury them horses so we can get back to town," Sul heard Armistead tell the other man. "Miss Catherine told me Marse Sul's — " he broke off. "What's that barn door doin' standin' open like that? I closed it when I left here earlier — " He started toward the barn door.

Sul leaped into his saddle and gathered Saber's reins. When Armistead opened the door, the boy yelled and kicked the roan forward.

With an echoing yell of surprise, Armistead jumped back as Sul and his horse flashed past him out the door, but his surprise didn't last. "Marse Sul," he shouted after the boy, "come back here, chile! Don't you know your ma's lookin' for you?"

Sul answered by heading Saber for the gate at a run. It wasn't until he rode clear of the wagon that he could see that Jake had closed it.

"We's got him now," the other man shouted gleefully.

"Good!" Armistead agreed behind him. "Grab his bridle!"

Jake tried. He lunged forward, snatching at Saber's reins. Sul swung the roan to one side and pulled the animal up onto his hind legs. Afraid of the slashing hoofs as the horse reared over him, Jake jumped backwards, tripped, and sat down.

Sul saw that Jake was up again in an instant, but by then he had Saber back down on all four feet and bounding for the gate. Not thinking of the danger but intent only on escape, the boy rammed Saber at the gate. He jumped the little horse over with only the narrowest clearance of the roan's rear hoofs over the top bar. Behind him he heard Armistead gasp at the reckless daring of the jump and then begin giving orders.

"You, Jake!" Armistead shouted. "Take that brown mule back to town an' tell Miss Catherine we spotted Marse Sul. I'm ridin' after him on this one!"

ON THE TRAIL

Saber wheeled around the yard fence into the lane, and Sul looked over his shoulder. Armistead was indeed unhitching one of the mules to come after him. The boy faced forward again with a grin. "Any time you can't outrun an old mule," he told the blue roan, "I'll trade you in on a terrapin myself! Let's go!" He leaned over Saber's neck and kicked the horse into a run.

As the roan sprang into a gallop beneath him, the boy heard Armistead wail, "Don't do this to your ma, Marse Sul!"

Sul only bent lower over Saber's rippling black mane and turned all his attention to leaving his would-be pursuer in the dust.

Sometime later, Sul slowed Saber to a trot and then finally to a walk. They were nearing a grove on the edge of the road which led to Barnard's North Bosque Trading Post and then to points west. "You did good, boy," he said, leaning forward to pat the roan's sweaty shoulder. "Thanks to you, we left Armistead and his mule behind us a long time ago. Let's get what we need from the trading post and then head west. I just hope this isn't one of the days George decides to check on his employees."

Fortunately, no one Sul knew was in sight when he rode into

the post about an hour before sundown. Near the warehouse a wagon was being loaded with hides and furs, but the men loading it were too busy to give him more than a glance. Trying to look as grownup as possible, the boy dismounted and tied Saber in the shade of a cottonwood tree before going into the trading house with his rifle, powder horn, and deerskin.

To the boy's relief, the trader showed no curiosity about him as he entered and presented the deerskin.

"Fifteen cents," the man said when he had examined the skin. "That's all I can give you, it bein' an uncured hide."

"I'll take it in powder to fill my horn, hard crackers, and bacon," Sul answered. He glanced around. "Any Delawares or Anadarkos been in lately?" he asked casually.

"No, but there were some Wacos and Caddos here earlier in the week." The trader took the powder horn and began to fill Sul's order. "The others don't come down here much since we opened our post up by Comanche Peak."

Sul blushed. He had forgotten that George Barnard had mentioned the new trading post the last time he had visited the family.

"Is it far for the Anadarkos to come?" the boy went on.

The trader snorted. "Naw, some of 'em just don't like askin' permission from the army to come within the new line of forts."

"No," Sul said, "I mean, is your new post far for them to come?"

"Only about as far as it is from here to Fort Graham," the man replied. He handed over the refilled powder horn, a slab of bacon, and a sack of crackers. "Say, haven't I seen you somewhere?" he asked belatedly.

Sul waved a vague hand in the direction of Waco. "My folks live back that way a piece, between here and the ferry," he said truthfully as he started to leave.

The trader nodded. "That must be it," he said and turned back to what he was doing when the boy came in.

With a sigh of relief, Sul closed the trading house door behind him and hurried to where he had left Saber tied. "So far so good," he told himself, stowing the bartered goods away and remounting.

As he cantered past the wagon on his way out, a young man with a bandaged ankle and leaning on a cane limped to the door of the warehouse. His eyes locked with Sul's, and the boy recognized the younger brother of Mary's suitor, George Barnard. What was worse, he realized, Charles Barnard had recognized him, too.

"You there — Sul Ross!" the young man roared behind him. "What are you doing here this time of day? Why aren't you at home in Waco?"

Sul's only answer was to kick Saber into another tearing gallop and put as much distance as possible between himself and the trading post.

Saber was beginning to breathe heavily when Sul slowed the blue roan's pace and twisted in his saddle to look back the way they had come. "There's nobody on our trail," he told the blowing horse, "so you can get your wind back." He dismounted, and going to Saber's head, stood there patting the blue's neck. "But I'll bet you a bucket of oats Charles Barnard lets them know in Waco that he's seen us. Drat, drat, drat!" As if in agreement, Saber tossed his head and then rubbed his nose on his master's sleeve.

The next morning Sul squatted over the small fire he had built and moved the sticks holding the sizzling strips of bacon closer to the flame. He had made a cold camp without a fire the evening before, eating for supper the biscuits and sweet potatoes he had brought with him from home. This morning he was hungry and ready for something warm, and he had decided to risk building a fire to cook the bacon. Behind him, Saber grazed at the end of his picket rope.

As he grilled the bacon, Sul tried to remember what he had

heard his father and his father's friend, Major Neighbors, tell about a trip they had taken up the Brazos into the Comanche Peak country two years before. As far as he could remember from the men's conversation, their party had gone up the east bank of the Brazos on their way to the Indian villages beyond. "But if I do that before I get to Fort Graham, there's a chance I could run into Hanse out on patrol or something," he told himself, reaching to remove his breakfast from the fire.

Sul was still pondering the problem when he put out the fire and broke camp some time later. "There's no help for it," he told Saber finally, as he pulled the roan's cinch tight. "We'll have to stay off the road and ride across country. From what Pa said, you can see Comanche Peak from fifty miles away, so we'll head for it. From there it will be easy to cut north to the Brazos."

Despite what his father had said, it was well after noon the next day when Sul trotted Saber up a slight rise and first spotted the long rampart of Comanche Peak lying on the northwestern horizon like a bank of low clouds. "There it is at last, boy," he said, pointing with his bridle hand. "From here it shouldn't be too far to the military road between Fort Gates and Fort Graham. Let's just hope we don't meet Hanse and a squad of the Dragoons out on a patrol."

Several miles farther on, they finally crossed the military road and dropped down the western side. "We've made it, boy," Sul said proudly, drawing rein well beyond the road. "This is the frontier at last. From now on we'll really be on our own." He stood up in his stirrups to look northwest of Comanche Peak. "Somewhere out there is the Brazos — and José María's village. We'll show Pa yet," he vowed.

Saber tossed his head and then pulled against the bit as if reaching for a clump of nearby prairie grass. Sul grinned and patted the blue's neck. "You're hungry and ready to stop, aren't you, boy? I'll start looking for a place for us to camp." Easing back down into his saddle, the boy urged the blue roan onward into a running walk. He did not know that at that same time, Pete was riding a tired horse onto the post at Fort Graham and stopping to ask the sentry on duty where he could find Sergeant Hanse Mason of I Company.

That afternoon Sul chose his campsite with special care as his father had taught him, tucking his horse, fire, and sleeping place back into the surrounding folds of a narrow gully branching off a larger ravine. Down the ravine a small water hole provided a drink for his mount and himself. "Now that we're beyond the military road, it's possible that any Indians we meet will be hostile unless we're lucky enough to run across some of José María's warriors," he told Saber as he pounded the roan's picket pin into the ground with a rock. "That means I've got to watch my back, build a low fire, and sleep with one eye open." He sat back on his heels and surveyed the mouth of the gully, nicely screened by two small cottonwood trees. "Even Pa would have trouble finding this place," he said with great satisfaction.

Picketing the blue with a shortened rope in a patch of good grass, Sul put some corn for the horse on his saddle blanket and took his rifle and Colt revolver out hunting for supper. A short distance from camp he flushed a prairie chicken out of the grass and got it with one shot.

Supper was simple: prairie chicken grilled over the glowing coals of the fire the boy smothered with dirt as soon as his meal was done. Then he wrapped himself in his saddle blanket and settled down to sleep, his rifle and revolver at hand. "I won't think of Ma and the others," he told himself resolutely. Just as he hung on the edge of sleep, however, Mervin's pale face did come to mind. "I hope you'll soon be well and strong, Merve," he said to himself.

It seemed Sul had been asleep only a minute or two when the howl of a nearby wolf jerked him into wakefulness. The boy sat up, his heart pounding, his hand closing instinctively on his revolver handle as a second howl answered the first. At the end of his picket rope, Saber moved uneasily. Sul started to speak to the blue, but before he could do so, he heard the sound of human voices. They were low, guttural, and nearby, and whatever language they spoke, it was not English. His heart in his throat, Sul jumped up and sprinted for the roan's head. Jamming the revolver into the waistband of his britches, he grabbed the animal's tie rope with one hand. With the other he grasped Saber's nostrils to keep him from whinnying.

For a long time he stood there listening, afraid to move and hardly to breathe, while he strained his hearing to learn if the Indians were coming any nearer. "Hope they haven't smelled my fire," he said to himself, grateful for the cottonwoods screening his campsite. At last the sounds of earthmuffled hoofbeats and more distant voices reached his ears. Whoever the party was, they were moving away, heading southwest.

Sul let his breath out cautiously, but he still kept his hand at Saber's nostrils. "Pa taught me what to do if I was ever captured by Indians," he told himself, "but I don't want to have to try it out." He continued to stand there, all senses alert, waiting, listening.

Saber nuzzled at his hand and tossed his head, anxious to begin eating again, but the boy was taking no chances. From the way the stars moved overhead, he judged a good three-quarters of an hour must have passed before he finally released the roan's nose. Then, getting his rifle and saddle blanket, he squatted near the horse to wait until dawn.

There were no other alarms the next night, although Sul still did not sleep well. After a breakfast of cold bacon and hard crackers washed down by water from a small stream nearby, he saddled Saber. "We should reach Comanche Peak by tomorrow, boy," he told the roan. "Then all we have to do is find the Brazos and follow it west."

As he rode away from his camp, Sul happened to look back the way they had come across a wide valley to a low chain of hills he had crossed the day before. Even at this distance he could see a black dot coming down the slope of the far hill.

His hand on the saddle horn, Sul stood again in his stirrups to try to make out what the dot was. "A rider!" he exclaimed finally, sinking back down. He gave Saber a nudge with his heels. "Come on, boy. Let's make tracks before whoever it is spots us!"

RIDE THE MAN DOWN

S ul rode on, and the country became more rolling. Every now and then he turned around to look back the way he had come, but there was no other sign of the rider he had spotted earlier. "He must not have had anything to do with us, boy," he said, urging the roan forward.

By mid morning, Comanche Peak was considerably closer. Even nearer was a swelling rise of prairie. "Look at that rise," Sul breathed to Saber. "I bet we can see for miles from that ridge. Let's head for the crest."

At the top of that rise he looked back once more. Sul gasped in surprise as the tiny figure of a horseman, closer than before and moving across a backdrop of prairie, caught his attention. "Look at that," he told the roan, "there *is* somebody on our back trail!"

For a moment Sul held steady, peering back at the rider, then he wheeled Saber and urged the blue roan over the crest of the rise. Some fifteen yards below the crest, Sul jerked his horse to a halt. "Stay here, boy, while I find out who it is," he said, picketing Saber. Taking his rifle and revolver, the boy ran back up the slope until he neared the top of the rise. Then he dropped to his stomach and bellied the rest of the way to the crest. When he first warily peered over, the horseman was hidden in a fold of the prairie.

"Come on," Sul said, bringing his rifle forward and cocking it, "show yourself."

His heart pounding in his ears, he waited until the rider reappeared on another swell of the prairie. This time the horseman was close enough for the boy to recognize the sorrel under the saddle — and the rider himself. "It's Hanse!" Sul groaned, flattening himself into the prairie grass. "That's not fair — they've sent Hanse after me!"

Uncocking his rifle, Sul rolled over onto his back and stared angrily up into the sky. "Why can't Ma and the others let me go?" he asked hotly. "Don't they know this is my chance at a new life away from Pa? And why did they have to bring Hanse into my adventure?" The boy's chest heaved. "Hanse might be the best white tracker Pa has ever run across," he told himself, "but I'll show him. I'll show them all!"

The next instant the boy rolled down below the crest, grabbed up his rifle, and ran for Saber. This time he did not speak to the roan but rather mounted and plunged down the far side of the rise. "They may have sent Hanse to ride us down, boy," he whispered to Saber as they gained the bottom and headed for a distant creek bed, "but we're going to give him a run for his money."

As he made a dash on Saber for the timber-lined creek bed about a quarter mile away, Sul blamed himself for neglecting to cover their tracks. "How could I be so stupid?" he groaned to himself. "We've left a trail a baby could follow. Hanse has been able to come right after us." Ahead of them, the creek bed offered cover, but there was not much water in the bottom of the cut as he turned Saber into the creek and headed northwest. "At least we're going the right way," Sul told himself as he rode on up the stream. Many of the rocks in the creek bed were loose underfoot, and he had to pull the blue roan down to a walking pace as the horse splashed nosily through the pools of water.

Twice Sul halted his horse and listened for sounds of pursuit. There were none, and he sighed in relief. "That's one for us," he whispered to Saber, patting the roan's sweaty neck. "If we can keep out of Hanse's way until dark, maybe we can still get away."

It was then he noticed that the sack containing his flint and steel, extra lead, and bullet mold had come untied and dropped off his saddle. "Where is it?" he muttered, looking back the way they had come. "I had it when we turned into the creek." For an instant Sul considered riding on without it; then he reined Saber sharply around and rode back the way he had come.

It took precious moments to retrace his trail. He had almost returned to the place where he had entered the creek before he spotted the sack lying on an outcrop of rock in the middle of the creek bed. Halting beside it, he vaulted from Saber's back to snatch it up and tie it to a saddle string. Then he remounted and turned Saber's nose once more toward the northwest. Behind him he heard the distant chink of horseshoe iron on stone.

"Hanse!" Sul exclaimed, kicking Saber in the ribs. "Let's go!"

This time he rode faster than he should have, and in one place Saber slipped on the rocks. As the blue roan fell into the water on one side, Sul threw himself out of the saddle, taking care to keep his rifle from getting wet. "Come on, boy," he cried, jerking on the reins, "you've got to get up!"

Saber tossed his head, fighting the bridle, but to Sul's relief, the blue was able to scramble unhurt to his feet. As the boy stepped back into the saddle he could hear, just around the next bend — or so it seemed — the sound of splashing, as if another horse was wading in the water of the creek. "Oh, no," Sul groaned and urged Saber forward.

Sul kept the blue roan to as fast a pace as he dared as they snaked back up the creek. Here the creek bed was smoother rock underfoot, but Saber was tiring as the cut widened and deepened. The boy looked around. Already the tops of the banks on either side were far above his head and the sides of the cut were too steep to ride out of safely. "Great — just great," he gritted, bending low over Saber's neck once more. "We'll have to keep going and hope we don't run into a box canyon or something."

About a quarter mile farther on, the boy turned a bend and realized his luck had run out. A short distance ahead the creek collected in a deep pool. Saber reared as Sul reined up on the brink. From the saddle he could look down into the pool's depths and see that although deep enough to dive into, the water was clogged with rocks.

"We've got to go back and hope we don't meet Hanse before we can climb out," Sul said, swinging Saber around and dashing back the way they had come. He stood up in the stirrups, scanning the creek banks for a place sloping enough for Saber to climb.

There was none, and he pushed on until he rounded a bend and rode into full open view of his pursuer.

"Sully!" Mason roared.

Sul swerved Saber to the side and heeled him up the creek bank. The incline was too steep for the animal to climb, and the roan balked and stumbled badly, sending the boy sprawling one way and his rifle spinning the other. Abandoning his horse, Sul leaped to his feet and bounded away. As he ran, he could hear Mason's horse plunging after him. He had run only a few yards when the sergeant cornered him.

"You young rip! What do you mean by runnin' off like that an' leavin' your ma in the lurch?" Mason demanded, backing him up against the creek bank with a stirrup in his ribs.

Sul ducked under the sorrel's neck and dashed off again. He heard an exclamation of anger and hoofbeats; the next instant he found himself snatched off his feet by his belt and braces and slung across the sorrel's shoulders in front of Mason's saddle.

"Hanse! Let me up!" Sul cried, his arms and legs flailing.

"Stay where you are, or I'll hogtie you," the sergeant ordered, twisting a hand in the boy's braces. "I ought to do it anyway, for all the trouble you've caused everybody."

Sul gulped then and stopped struggling. Hanse always meant what he said. "I'll be good," he answered meekly.

Mason nodded. "That's better." His hand still at Sul's back, the sergeant walked his horse to where the boy's rifle lay on the ground, dismounted, and retrieved the weapon. Then he took Saber's reins and tied them to his own saddle. Finally he grabbed Sul by the belt and pulled him off the horse onto his feet. A hand on each shoulder, he spun the boy around so that he could look him in the eyes. "Just where do you think you're goin'?" he demanded.

The boy put up his chin. "I'm running away."

"I can see that," Mason said. "Where you headin' — California?"

Sul answered scornfully. "No! It's a secret, and you'd tell Pa."

Mason's expression did not change. "Don't you think your pa'd care?" he asked.

"Not as long as he's got Pete around. He says I'm only fit to be a farmer!" The recollection of his father's words angered Sul once more. "I don't ever want to see Pa again," he added, his face hard.

"What about your ma?"

Sul allowed his expression to soften, but he didn't relent. "She's got the others. She won't miss me."

"That's not true," Mason said sharply. "She was worried that you'd get into trouble an' sent me after you."

"That figures," Sul answered, shrugging. "Pa wouldn't worry. To him I'm nothing but a money-maker."

"You know better than that," Mason told him. "Right now your pa doesn't know, an' your ma wasn't goin' to tell him until later."

The boy shrugged again. "I really don't care," he said, trying to appear unconcerned.

Mason's eyes gleamed. "Well, I do, an' I'm takin' you back like your ma asked."

Sul raised his chin a shade higher. "There's a lot of miles between here and Waco," he said.

The sergeant nodded. "An' it's up to you how you cross 'em. You can give me your parole that you won't try to run away an' ride back home like a rational bein' or you can be hauled back tied to your saddle. Either way is all right with me, but it's your choice. I warn you right here an' now — you try to give me the slip an' I'll take you home slung over my saddlebow like a papoose on a cradleboard." He paused. "Now, what do you have to say for yourself?"

"Nothing," Sul answered. "I ran away. You caught me. I'm your prisoner, Hanse, but I don't have to like it. And I'm not going to give you my parole."

If possible, the sergeant's dark eyes gleamed more fiercely than ever at this defiance. "Never bet against a sure thing, young'un," he said softly, stepping into his saddle. "An' the sure thing is that I'm goin' to return you to Waco." He gestured toward Saber. "Mount up. We'll find a place close by where we can camp an' graze the horses. You an' that roan of yours both look like you could use some rest."

That evening Sul, his knees drawn up to his chin and his arms folded around his knees, sat watching the flames of their camp-fire while his companion prepared their supper.

"That's the last of the bacon," Mason said from across the fire, rubbing his greasy hands on a tuft of prairie grass. "It'll be hunter's luck tomorrow after we finish them crackers." He looked over at the boy, and his harsh face softened. "You want to talk about it?" he asked.

Sul shook his head.

"Well, just remember that when you do, you can talk to me about anythin' — anythin'."

"I know." Sul stared back at the fire as he waited for the bacon to cook. Once or twice he caught himself dozing and had to jerk himself awake. "I can't fall asleep," he told himself fiercely. "That's something a baby would do." Suddenly he saw his sleepiness as a chance for one last break for freedom. "If I can only convince Hanse I'm really sleepy, maybe I can sneak away tonight after he's fallen asleep." The boy felt a thrill of excitement once he had decided on action. "That should really show Pa if I can get away from Hanse," he told himself.

Noticing Mason was studying him, Sul yawned widely and allowed his eyelids to droop even more.

"Why don't you turn in as soon as supper is over?" the sergeant suggested.

Sul smiled to himself, nodded, and began making his plans.

Several hours later, Sul threw back the flap of blanket covering his face and listened. They had bedded down right after supper, Hanse on one side of their dead fire, himself on the other. Wrapped in his blanket, the sergeant lay on his side, turned away from the fire. His breathing seemed deep and regular.

The boy grinned and sat up, pushing back his own blanket. He waited a few minutes, still listening, before rising stealthily to his feet. He got his own weapons and blanket and carried them on tiptoe to a place nearer the horses, and then he came back and bent to heft his saddle.

As Sul lifted it, Mason raised himself on one elbow. "Goin' somewhere, young'un?" he asked.

ON THE PLAINS

Chief jumped a washed-out place in the prairie hillside, and Sul, slung as promised across the front of Mason's saddle, jounced uncomfortably. Riding that way hadn't been too bad when they first started that morning, but now, after a couple of miles, he was getting sick at his stomach.

He looked back at Saber, following along behind the sorrel. "We're two of a kind," Sul thought miserably, remembering the rope Mason had tied around his waist and then attached to the sorrel's saddle. "Even if I did jump off, I couldn't run away. And the knot's in the back, so I can't reach it." He glanced back over his shoulder, trying unsuccessfully to see the sergeant's harsh face as Mason spurred his mount into a trot. As Chief's pace became faster and rougher, Sul felt a decided unsettledness in his midsection.

"I'm going to puke," he said out loud, putting his hand to his mouth.

"Go ahead an' puke," his captor answered unfeelingly, without slowing their pace.

Sul tried to choke it back, gagged, and vomited down Chief's shoulder. "I told you so," he said reproachfully when he could speak again.

"An' I told you what I was goin' to do if you tried to give me the slip," Mason retorted. He put his sorrel into an even rougher trot.

Wretchedly, Sul vomited again. "Please, Hanse — " he begged, gagging.

Mason slowed his horse. "Give me your parole that you won't try to run away again," he ordered.

Sul sighed. "I promise," he said.

"That's better." The sergeant stopped his horse and allowed the boy to slide down to stand beside the animal. "I figured you'd rather ride home upright." He bent from the saddle to untie the knot at Sul's back and then freed Saber's reins. "You can mount up," he said, handing them to the boy, "but if you break your word to me, I'll hogtie you an' haul you all the way home that way."

"You won't have to," Sul answered, climbing into his saddle. For the first time, he grinned at his captor. "But you've got to admit, Hanse, it would have been something if I had been able to get away from you."

Mason shook his head. "You wouldn't have gotten far. An' it was bad thinkin', young'un, to run off in the first place an' leave a superior force that could mount a pursuit in your rear."

"That wasn't fair, calling you in," Sul said. "I'd already out-smarted Pete and Armistead."

Mason put his horse into motion. "I would have caught you anyway, because I guessed you were headin' for José María's village on the Brazos. Ain't I right?"

Sul's grin vanished. "How did you know?" he asked stiffly, trotting Saber alongside Mason's sorrel.

"I remembered your pa an' me talkin' about it that night with you just in earshot," the sergeant explained. "Besides, you were easy enough to trace once I knew which way you were headed, because your trail led straight out here. You could've covered your tracks better than that, young'un."

Sul slumped in his saddle. "I know," he admitted. "I realized that after I noticed we were being followed. Hanse, have you ever wanted something so bad you could almost taste it?"

"Lots of times, young'un," the sergeant answered. "I wanted my ma an' pa mighty bad after that raidin' party killed 'em an' carried me off. An' I really wanted Greta an' our little girls when they died of yellow fever. For a long time I wished I could have died with 'em."

"But you lived anyway," Sul pointed out.

"I lived," Mason agreed. "What is it you want so bad?"

Sul paused before answering, reluctant to reveal even to this good friend the hurt that he felt, but at last he spoke. "I heard Pa that night," he said quietly. "He's going to get Pete an appointment to West Point — Pete!" The boy's tone was suddenly scornful. "He wants to be a soldier, but not as much as I do." He looked hopefully at Mason. "There couldn't be two appointments from the same family, could there?"

"I don't reckon so, young'un, but you don't have to graduate from West Point to be a soldier," the sergeant answered. "I've known a lot of good officers who've either come up through the ranks or in by direct commission. You could do the same. When I got leave to come after you, I told my captain you had the makin's of one of the finest natural Dragoon officers I'd ever seen."

The boy's tense face lightened. "Do you mean that?" he asked. "You aren't just saying that because of what Pa did, are you?"

"Have I ever lied to you, young'un?" Mason replied.

Sul shook his head. "Not that I know of."

The sergeant went on. "I mean it all right. Besides, your pa sayin' he's goin' to get Pete an appointment an' gettin' one are two different things. You should know that."

The boy nodded. "But I want more schooling too — I could get both if I went to West Point."

"You could get more schoolin' even if you didn't," Mason said. "Make your own luck, young'un."

"But how, Hanse? Pa's determined to make a farmer out of me — and he hasn't farmed regular in his life. He's too restless to do anything for long," Sul added bitterly. "But he said farming was all I was fit for."

The sergeant frowned. "Young'un, your pa didn't mean for you to hear all that."

"Then he shouldn't have said it. But you know Pa — he says what he thinks at all times." Sul rode in silence for a short distance before turning back to his companion. "Hanse, what should I do? Pa's wrong — I've got it in me to be more than just a farmer. I know it!"

"An' you wanted him to know it, too," the sergeant ventured. "Is that why you ran off?"

Sul grinned. "A good part of the reason," he admitted and then instantly sobered. "Pa plays favorites," he said slowly. "You know he does."

The sergeant nodded. "I know, young'un. He always has. I told your pa to his face that he was makin' a big mistake plannin' your future like that, but I don't reckon he's listenin' right now. What else?"

"Twice Pa hided me for something I didn't do."

"Pete told me about that," Mason said.

Sul went on. "He wouldn't listen to me — "

"You know how your pa gets when he's mad," Mason answered.

"Well, he made me mad, too, Hanse," Sul replied, "so mad I didn't ever want to see Pa again. And I still don't," he added hotly. "At least not yet."

"You'll get over it," Mason told him matter-of-factly. To Sul's relief, the sergeant said nothing more on the subject.

They rode in silence for about five minutes; then Sul sighed deeply. "If only I looked like Pa instead of Ma's side of the family — " he began.

"You still would be the second son, Sully, not the first, an'

nothin' short of Pete dyin' is goin' to change that," Mason pointed out. "You don't want that, do you?"

"No, I don't," Sul said. "Pete's all right as an older brother. But
why does he get along with Pa and I can't?"

"You're too much like your pa — that's why," Mason told him.

Puzzled, Sul asked, "What do you mean?"

The sergeant shifted in his saddle before answering. "Pete's
different, see — he looks like your pa, but he don't act like him.
That's why they don't clash. Now you an' your pa — you don't
look alike, but you are alike in a lot of ways." He glanced at the
boy before going on. "From what your pa told me once, he ran
away a couple of times when he was a young'un because of the
way he was treated at home."

"Oh," Sul said, "I didn't know that." He paused thoughtfully
while he considered this information.

"Anythin' else?" Mason asked.

"Well, I don't like being the runt of the family," Sul protested. "Pete's going to be tall — like Pa." He paused again. "I don't
know about Mervin and Bob," he admitted.

"You don't like bein' the runt? Well, I don't like bein' thought
a half-breed, either," Mason retorted, "but there ain't much we
can do about it. Still, there's a lot you can do for yourself, Sully
— includin' gettin' your own schoolin'."

Sul sighed once more, this time with more contentment.
Suddenly it didn't seem quite so bad to be heading home, even
if he didn't want to see his father yet. "Thanks, Hanse," he said.
"I think I will." As if waking from a dream, the boy looked
around them and at the sun on his right hand. "We're headed
northwest," he said, pointing. "That's not the way back to
Waco."

The sergeant smiled briefly at him. "I figured that as long as
we're out this way, we'd drop by José María's village before
startin' back," he said. "It won't take us but a day or so out of our
way."

Sul beamed. "Thanks. I didn't like to go back without at least seeing it. But won't you get in trouble at the fort?"

"When I asked for leave to come after you, the captain said take as much time as I needed to get you straightened out," the sergeant explained. "Besides, we've heard rumors that Seminoles from the Creek Nation are travelin' from village to village, tryin' to talk the wild tribes into breakin' the treaty we have with 'em. An' you know what that'll mean."

"War all along the frontier," the boy said soberly. "That's bad news."

"Plenty bad for everybody concerned," Mason agreed. "The captain said that if I got a chance to talk to any of the chiefs while I was out here I was to take it. So I'm goin' to start with José María."

"I hope the rumors aren't true, but I'll be glad to visit the Anadarkos." Sul waved his arms widely. "This is going to be a good adventure after all," he said happily, determined to enjoy his freedom as long as it lasted. "How soon do you think we'll get there?"

"It's a good day's ride," the sergeant answered. "What's the matter — you gettin' hungry?"

"Hungry's not the word for it, now that my stomach is settling down," Sul admitted. He waited for Mason to tell him to tighten his belt another notch, but this time the sergeant really did smile.

"Let's see if we can get us an antelope," he suggested. "It'd be good manners to bring somethin' into José María's village with us this evenin'."

However, antelope seemed in short supply that morning although they spent some time actively hunting. Just before noon they were able to bag a quartet of prairie chickens, each one of them getting a pair of the birds on the wing.

"Good shootin', Sully," Mason said, dismounting to retrieve the birds. "These will be better than nothin'. There's a creek up ahead where we can stop. While I get 'em ready to cook, you collect firewood an' start a fire."

A little later, their noon meal was broiling over the fire. Sul had gone for more wood and had come back with his arms loaded when he realized Mason was looking intently back the way they had come.

"What is it, Hanse?" he asked.

The sergeant's expression did not change. "Comanches," he said quietly. "There's a couple of 'em on the next rise, watchin' us."

COMANCHES

Sul's mouth was suddenly dry. "Are they friendly?" he asked.
"Don't know, but I reckon we'll soon find out," Mason told
him. "In the meantime, don't make any sudden moves. Be
ready to fight if we have to, though."

Acting as naturally as possible, Sul set the firewood down and
turned so he could put his hand on the handle of his revolver
without being seen. "I'm ready," he said.

Mason's eyes glowed in approval. "Good. I think they're Chief
Ketumse's warriors an' friendly. Stay sharp until we know for
sure."

Sul nodded. As he watched, he saw the sergeant make the
sign for peace and then the welcoming sign. Beyond them, the
foremost of the two riders also made the friendship sign and then
some signs Sul did not recognize. "What are they saying,
Hanse?" he whispered.

"They're askin' to come to our fire," the sergeant replied in a
low voice. "I'm goin' to tell 'em to come on. You stay in the
background an' let me deal with 'em. An' don't let 'em know I
speak Comanche."

Sul nodded again and stepped back. To his surprise, as the two young warriors leading an extra horse approached them, the one riding in front spoke to Mason in English.

"Laughing Boy," the younger of the two warriors said, pointing to himself. Indicating his companion who was leading the extra horse loaded with the carcass of an antelope, he added, "Tall Horse. We have meat; we share."

"Laughin' Boy an' Tall Horse are welcome at our fire," the sergeant said, speaking in English but also making the signs. "Their meat is welcome too. I, Far Eyes, thank you."

It seemed to Sul that Mason was waiting to see if the newcomers would respond to his Indian name. Apparently it meant nothing to the pair. Indeed, the younger warrior's eyes glinted mockingly when the sergeant so identified himself.

"We greet you, Far Eyes — " Laughing Boy said; then he paused and looked more closely at Sul before going on in English, " — and little Sky Eyes. What do you do here?"

"We seek the village of José María," Mason answered. "The boy here wants to see how the Anadarkos live."

Laughing Boy smiled. "You want see how men live, you seek villages my people."

"The villages of the People are harder to find," Mason said. He turned to Sul. "Put some more wood on the fire, young'un, an' get it good an' hot. I've got a feelin' Laughin' Boy an' Tall Horse are goin' to give us a feast."

Without speaking, Sul bent to do as the sergeant asked. Again he could feel the eyes of the two Comanches upon him, and as he worked around the campfire, he moved quietly and carefully to show no signs of nervousness or fear.

"Little Sky Eyes wears little pistol," Laughing Boy said when cuts of antelope were at last grilling on the fire. He pointed to Sul's Colt, and the boy saw that the young warrior was wearing a pair of heavy silver bracelets. "You shoot it?" the Comanche asked.

The boy looked at Mason, who nodded. Sul took that as permission to answer the question. "As good as a man," he said, facing the Comanche proudly.

Laughing Boy clapped his hands. "Little Sky Eyes big warrior some day," he said. Again his eyes glinted mockingly.

Sul knew the Comanche was teasing him, but the young warrior seemed so good-natured about it that it didn't bother him. He grinned at Laughing Boy, who turned and spoke in Comanche to his friend. Tall Horse replied, saying something which caused the younger man to laugh, and then Laughing Boy began to talk in sign language to Mason. Sul caught something about five horses, but the signs were made so rapidly he could not read them all.

When the Comanche had finished, the sergeant shook his head and made the negation sign. "He is my *tua*," he said in English.

Laughing Boy grinned and repeated the negation sign. "Sky Eyes is *tua* of Far Eyes," he agreed. "Far Eyes sees far, sees Kickapoo warriors this place and river?"

Mason showed no concern. He removed the meat from the fire before answering. "How many warriors?" he asked finally.

"We see six — more ride far. Not all return," Laughing Boy answered, his eyes sparkling like he knew a good joke. He looked over at Sul. "Little Sky Eyes fears Kickapoos?"

"No more than he does Comanches," Mason answered. "Come an' eat. The meat is ready."

Sometime later, Laughing Boy raised one braceleted arm and waved as he and Tall Horse rode off. Sul returned the wave. It was only after he had done so that he realized that Mason had come to stand behind him.

"What did you think of that?" the sergeant asked.

"I kind of liked Laughing Boy," Sul replied, grinning. He turned to face the older man. "He seemed like a lot of fun."

"Did you now?" Mason looked closely at him. "He was sure taken with you," the sergeant said. "Offered me five horses for you, but I told him you were the same as my nephew."

Sul gasped. "Why would he do that?"

"Your blue eyes — an' your spunk," Mason explained. "They're always lookin' for boys they can adopt an' raise as warriors."

Sul nodded. "Like they did you," he said.

"Like they did me," Mason agreed. "An' you've got to admit, young'un, blue eyes an' black hair ain't that common even among white folks. I doubt if them two Comanches have ever seen anybody like you. The young one kept talkin' about your blue eyes."

"So that's why he called me 'Sky Eyes,'" Sul said. "But you were friendly with him, Hanse."

The sergeant nodded shortly. "Real friendly. But I didn't tell him my name in Comanche or yours either. An' I didn't talk to 'em in Comanche."

"I wondered about that," Sul admitted.

"Figured I could learn a lot more about what they're plannin' if I didn't," Mason explained. "When you're dealin' with Comanches, it pays to leave yourself an ace or two in the hole."

"You told them where we were going," Sul pointed out.

"I did that to give 'em a reason for us bein' out here. Otherwise they might have figured we're up to no good an' followed us." The sergeant laid one hand on Sul's shoulder. "If you ever find yourself around Comanches older than them two who just left, tell 'em you're the tua of Gray Wolf's white son, He-Who-Sees-Far. That should give you some protection." He jerked his head in the direction the pair had gone. "Them two are too young to remember me, but the older men'll recognize the name."

Startled, Sul asked, "Hanse, you didn't overhear something, did you?"

"Nothin' but Laughin' Boy goin' on about your courage an'

blue eyes. But he's plenty sharp an' might have figured I knew more Comanche than I was lettin' on." The sergeant turned and kicked dirt on their fire. "Let's get ready to ride."

Sul went to Saber. "Do you think it's true about the Kickapoos?" he asked as they rode away from their campsite. "Laughing Boy's eyes sure shone when he told us about them."

"That horse they're leadin' is saddled with Kickapoo equip-ment," the sergeant answered. "More than likely he an' Tall Horse have already taken some Kickapoo scalps. We'll keep our eyes peeled."

As they rode northwest side by side, angling toward the Brazos, Sul stayed alert. He noticed that Mason was watch-ful too, his eyes continually scanning the prairie around them. More time passed, though, and the boy began to relax — and think about something that was still bothering him. "Hanse," he said finally as they rode on through the tall prairie grass, "did Pete tell you what the sheriff of Milam County did?"

"No," Mason said. "What happened?"

Sul repeated the story and then asked, "Why didn't he keep his word? He promised me he'd tell Pa."

"There could have been a lot of reasons why he didn't, young'un. But you'd better learn now that there'll be folks that you can't depend on — who'll let you down. You savvy?"

The boy nodded slowly, and the sergeant went on. "What about yourself? Why did you do what you did?"

Sul considered before speaking. "First of all, I didn't want that fellow getting off with Red Rover if he had really stolen him," he said.

"That makes sense. Anythin' else?"

Sul glanced sideways at his friend. "For the adventure, I guess. I wanted to see if I could outsmart that fellow. And I did, too!"

"An' show off for your pa?" Mason asked.

"That, too," Sul admitted. "I wanted Pa to be proud of me. That's why it hurt when the sheriff didn't keep his word and tell Pa I'd helped him."

"He probably didn't like thinkin' he owed any help to a young'un like you," Mason pointed out. "Just remember, Sully — if you ever reach a position of authority yourself, don't forget the little folks that helped you get there. Each one of us owes somethin' to somebody else."

"Even you?" Sul asked.

Hanse nodded. "Old Miz Mason for one. Greta for another. An' your pa an' ma. Even Gray Wolf — "

He broke off as a party of five braves with crested scalplocks burst out of cover on their right and galloped toward them, shooting and yelling.

"Kickapoos!" Mason yelled at Sul. "Ride for that creek up ahead! An' don't return their fire until we're safe in cover!"

Sul kicked Saber into a run. As the blue roan bounded forward, the boy looked back to see that the sergeant had drawn his own revolver and turned his sorrel in to ride behind him. Almost level with them on this dash for timber, the Kickapoo war party yelled louder and began shooting their bows. One arrow passed harmlessly between Sul's shoulder and Saber's ears while another nicked the boy's right forearm.

Behind him Mason fired a couple of shots at the Kickapoos, and then there was the "thonk" of an arrow hitting muscle. Sul glanced back to see a feathered shaft still quivering in the back of the sergeant's right shoulder. "Hanse!" he screamed.

"It's all right!" Mason yelled. "Do like I told you. We've got better horses — we can outrun 'em!" He fired again at their pursuers.

Sul gritted his teeth and bent closer over Saber's neck. It was hard to ride this way without returning any of the Kickapoos' fire. His trigger finger itched to be shooting like Hanse was, but he followed orders. As they reached the cover of the trees beside the stream, Sul jumped from the blue's back and ducked behind a tree. He was on one knee and firing his rifle at the nearest warrior when Mason joined him. To the boy's great satisfaction, the Kickapoo dropped his weapon. Although the warrior did not fall, he swayed as if wounded and turned his horse out of the fight.

"Now use your Colt," the sergeant ordered, reloading his own weapon. "They ain't expectin' you to have one too."

Sul nodded, and taking careful aim, fired at the remaining warriors. His first shot hit one of the attackers' horses. The animal went down, spilling its rider. By his third shot Mason was shooting again too. One of the Kickapoos tumbled from his horse, and the rest of them swerved their mounts aside, turning out of range. Mason yelled after them in Comanche. That ended the attack. Collecting their wounded and dismounted companions, the Kickapoos quickly rode away from the creek.

"Better reload," the sergeant directed.

"Do you think they'll be back?" Sul asked, reaching for his powder flask.

"Not if they understand Comanche an' have got any sense. I told 'em our brothers among the People are on the lookout for more Kickapoo scalps."

"Laughing Boy and Tall Horse." Sul grinned but instantly sobered. "You're hurt. That arrow — "

Mason nodded. "You'll have to pull it out for me. I can't reach it myself."

Sul shrank back. "Hanse, I can't!"

"You can! I can't pull it out without riskin' leavin' the head in the wound, so you'll have to do it. Besides, if you're goin' to be a soldier, you'd better get used to wounds an' death. An' it won't hurt for you to know a little somethin' about pain, either. Maybe then you'll think twice before puttin' your men in a place where you can get 'em killed or wounded." He frowned at the boy.

"Take the shaft an' pull up on it while you're rollin' it between your hands. That'll bring it out."

"But that'll hurt — " Sul began.

"Sure it'll hurt," Mason agreed, "but that's the best way, young'un. I'd do the same to you if I had to. Now do it!"

Flinching at the pain he was causing, Sul removed the arrow as the sergeant directed. By the time he had bandaged the wound with a torn piece of shirt, his hand was shaking.

"That's good enough for now," Mason said. "We'll treat it later. Right now we'd better clear out just in case them Kickapoos come back."

"But can you ride?" Sul protested. "The way you bled when I pulled the arrow out — "

"I can ride," the sergeant said gruffly. He reached out with his left hand and took the boy's arm. "Roll up your sleeve," he ordered. When Sul did so, he asked, "Why didn't you say you'd been hit too?"

"You always told me a good officer looks after his men and horses first," Sul said. "But I forgot about it, Hanse. Honest. It doesn't hurt all that much."

"All right — we'll take care of it later. An' one of the first rules of bein' a good officer is to look after your men first," Mason admitted, going to his sorrel. "But you're proud of that scratch too, I'll be bound," he added, mounting.

Sul grinned appealingly. "Pete's never been wounded by an arrow," he said.

"Figured you'd look at it that way," Mason said. "Ride ahead of me up the creek," he directed. "We'll keep to the water a ways in case they come back."

Several miles on, another tree-lined stream offered shelter, water, and the medicinal plants Mason needed to treat both their injuries. Sul helped him by tying a fresh bandage around his shoulder.

The boy frowned at the bloodstains on the bandage he had just removed. "Hanse, can't we stop here awhile? We haven't seen any more of the Kickapoos, and I could graze the horses while you get some sleep. You lost a lot of blood."

"Still lookin' after your troops?" Mason asked. "All right, young'un, I trust you to stand guard while I let that poultice work. Only you call me right away if you hear or see anythin' I should know about. Wake me by sundown anyway."

Sul beamed with pride at this faith in his abilities. "I will," he promised.

The rest of the afternoon passed uneventfully although Mason slept more heavily than Sul had expected. A couple of hours before sundown the boy moved the horses to another patch of grass nearby. As he pounded Saber's picket pin into the ground, an emptiness in his stomach reminded him that at home it would soon be suppertime.

"There's a pecan tree just around that next bend," he told Saber, patting the blue's neck. "I'll walk down there and see if I can pick up any of last year's pecans. Maybe that will hold me until time to get Hanse up." Leaning his rifle carefully against a tree, Sul trotted down the creek toward the pecan tree.

As he had hoped, he found nuts from the last year's crop scattered on the ground under the tree and was able to fill his pockets. He had started back to where he had left Hanse and the horses when he heard a rustle in the bushes to his left.

Sul whirled to learn what was making the sound. There was nothing that he could see, but before he could take another step forward, he was grabbed from behind. A bare arm was thrown across his chest, pinning his arms, and a hand was clamped over his mouth. Even in that instant of danger, Sul recognized the silver bracelets worn by Laughing Boy.

"We will not hurt you, little Sky Eyes," Laughing Boy whispered in his ear, and Sul could see then that Tall Horse was standing nearby. "Come to our village — we will show you how the People live." He said something in his own language to Tall Horse and held the boy tighter as the other Comanche stepped forward with a rawhide rope in one hand.

Sul's answer was to aim a well-placed kick into Tall Horse's groin. As the older warrior folded in the middle like a jackknife, Sul heard Laughing Boy crow with laughter. This amusement was cut short when he bit the hand over his mouth as hard as he could and stomped on the Comanche's moccasined toes. With a wrench, he twisted free of Laughing Boy's grasp.

"Han — !" he started to yell, but his cry was cut off in mid word by a blow to the side of the head. The impact sent him spinning to the ground, and as Sul went down, he found himself falling headlong into a well of unconsciousness.

CAPTURED

Sul opened his eyes as the horse beneath him jumped a narrow stream cut and loped forward again. His head hurt and his stomach churned, but from the sour taste in his mouth he had already vomited. For an instant the boy swayed, grasping the animal's mane with his bound hands, but a firm arm around his waist kept him from falling.

Raising his head dizzily, he wondered how he came to be riding double on a strange horse that was neither Saber nor Chief. Then, as his head cleared, he saw Tall Horse riding ahead of him, leading the extra horse, and realized that the arm around his waist wore silver bracelets. "Now I remember," Sul said to himself with a thrill of excitement. "I've been captured by Comanches!"

His next thought was for Hanse. "I want my uncle," he said out loud, struggling to sit up. "If you have killed him, I will shoot you myself." It was an empty boast, he knew, for he had left his rifle behind and they had probably taken his Colt from him, but Pa had always taught him Indians were impressed by courage.

"Little Sky Eyes will be big warrior some day," Laughing Boy repeated good-humoredly without moving his arm. "Then we give him knife and little pistol."

Sul nodded to himself. So they had taken his weapons. But what about Hanse — what had happened to him? Had the Comanches killed him while he slept? "I want my uncle," he said again.

The young warrior went on. "We did not kill uncle. Far Eyes has horses and scalp." With a laugh, the Comanche released his grip so that Sul could sit up. "He's shamed — we have *tua*."

"No!" His eyes blazing at this mocking of his hero, Sul twisted around to face his captor. He intended to blurt out what the sergeant had told him about his relationship to Gray Wolf but suddenly thought better of it. That time would come later. Right now it was best if these Comanches thought Hanse was no threat. Otherwise they might go back and kill him. Instead the boy said, "You have shamed me! I gave my word to Far Eyes that I would not run away, and you have made me a liar. My honor is shamed! And," he added accusingly, "you said you would not hurt me." He didn't know how much Laughing Boy would understand, but he hoped his courage would impress the warrior.

"You call Far Eyes — we kill Far Eyes," the Comanche explained. "Plenty honor to steal *tua* from bluecoat soldier. Like counting coup — brave deed like touching live enemy in battle."

Sul shook his head. "You have shamed my honor," he repeated. He motioned with his hands. "Untie me."

It was Laughing Boy's turn to shake his head. "We watch Far Eyes and Sky Eyes fight Kickapoos — see Sky Eyes *muy bravo*. Want adopt him into our band. Tall Horse made sure you do not run away — tie hands." He smiled at Sul. "If honor of Sky Eyes so great, why give word he not run away?"

Sul ducked his head. "I ran away from home," he admitted, "because my father beat me. Far Eyes was taking me back."

"Father will not beat Sky Eyes now," Laughing Boy pointed out. He grinned at Sul. "No see father again — Sky Eyes be my *tua*, live in my tepee. We go to the village now."

"But I want to see my father again!" Sul blurted out. That answer surprised even himself.

Laughing Boy had no answer to that, and their talk ceased. That gave Sul a chance to look around and try to decide which direction they were riding and how long it had been since his capture. He saw that the sun was only about an hour later down the sky. And from the position of Comanche Peak, he knew they were heading south.

After gaining these bearings, the boy relaxed and leaned back against his captor. "Hanse will come after me," he told himself confidently, "I know he will. And when he sees I've left Saber and my rifle behind he'll know I didn't go off on my own." Then another comforting thought came to mind, and he smiled to himself.

Laughing Boy, however, had seen it. "Change your mind?" the young warrior asked hopefully. "Not want to see father again?"

Sul shook his head once more and answered honestly. "I was thinking that Pete, my brother, has never seen a village of the People before, much less been captured by them."

They rode on through the twilight and into the night, keeping as much as possible to the rocky stream and riverbeds. Far too excited to sleep, Sul tried to judge their direction and the passage of time by the movement of the stars overhead. For a while before moonrise he considered his chances of getting away should he be able to slip off the horse and dart off into the darkness, but at last he gave it up. "Laughing Boy's too alert," he told himself. "Even if I could jump down, I wouldn't get very far. I wish I had something to mark our trail with, though."

Toward morning, when the moon had gone behind a cloud bank and they rode in darkness through a dry stream cut, Sul was able to unbuckle his knife belt and let it drop off his waist to the ground. "If Hanse finds it, he'll know we passed this way," he told himself. "I just hope Laughing Boy doesn't notice it's missing until it's too late to go back looking for it."

As it was, Tall Horse was the one who noticed the belt was gone when they stopped briefly at daybreak. Pointing at Sul's waist, the older warrior spoke angrily to Laughing Boy.

The younger warrior looked keenly at his captive, his eyes gleaming in such a way Sul felt the Comanche knew what he had done. Before Laughing Boy could speak, Sul brought up the subject himself.

"If you're wondering where my belt is," he said coolly, returning the Comanche's searching look, "it fell off — a long way back." Raising his chin, the boy then added, "It's too far to go back after it."

To Sul's relief, Laughing Boy chuckled. "*Tua* speaks the truth," he said. "Too far — we ride on." His eyes sparkling, the younger Comanche untied the rope on the boy's wrists and motioned for him remove his boots and socks.

"What do you want?" Sul asked, pretending not to understand.

Laughing Boy did not answer him. Turning to his friend, the young warrior spoke to Tall Horse. Sul heard the other Comanche give a short laugh before coming to pull the boots and socks off for him and hand them to Laughing Boy.

Sul glared at the two Comanches, but inside he felt shaky. Pa had warned him that Indians would sometimes strip their captives to prevent their escape. Would they take his clothes as well? "Why do you take my boots?" he asked as boldly as he dared.

"So *Tua* not run away," Laughing Boy repeated, tying the boots together and slinging them across the shoulders of his horse in front of him. Then he grinned mockingly at the boy and made signs for him to mount the extra horse.

This time Sul did as he was told but not without protest. "I won't run away," he said scornfully. "Give me back my boots. I need them."

Laughing Boy ignored his demand. "Ride ahead," the Comanche ordered. Then his face and voice hardened. "Something more 'fall off' we will take clothes too," he warned.

Sul could feel himself blushing at this threat, but he decided to ignore his embarrassment and continue his bold stance, like his father had always taught him. He straightened himself proudly in the saddle. "It is not right that you shame your *tua* in this way," he said coolly, urging the horse forward.

Laughing Boy's eyes gleamed appreciatively. "Sky Eyes will be big warrior some day," he said once more.

That afternoon Sul squatted on his bare heels in the shade cast by the extra horse and munched a piece of dried meat given him by Laughing Boy. He was both hungry and sleepy, but this was the first time the Comanches and their captive had halted for any length of time.

Tall Horse, who was acting as lookout for their party, said something to Laughing Boy in Comanche and pointed back the way they had come. Sul looked that way, wondering if it could be Mason, but immediately realized the rider was another warrior.

"Kiowa," Laughing Boy replied, and then he added some other words the boy did not understand. The young warrior did not seem pleased to see the newcomer. Tall Horse likewise appeared tense.

Curious for his first close view of one of the fierce allies of the Comanches, Sul shoved the rest of the meat into his shirt pocket and got to his feet. He was standing quietly, waiting beside the extra horse as the other warrior rode up.

Older than either of Sul's two captors, the Kiowa wore his hair in knee-length braids and carried a lance and shield. His pride was evident by the way he spoke arrogantly to the two younger warriors. Then, suddenly, he saw the boy standing there. The Kiowa's face twisted. Waving his lance, he pointed at Sul and then shouted at the two Comanche warriors. There was no need to speak the Kiowa's language to recognize the anger and hatred in his voice.

"He would like to kill me," Sul said to himself with a stab of fear. Remembering what his father had taught him — that he should never show pain or fear to an Indian — he stood prouder and taller and looked unwaveringly at the Kiowa.

Laughing Boy answered the newcomer, speaking loudly. He too motioned toward Sul. The argument went on. Sul thought he heard the Comanche word *tua* again; then the Kiowa yelled and kicked his horse forward. He jabbed his lance into the ground at Sul's feet and screamed what could only be a curse. The boy stood his ground, returning the man's angry glare with what he hoped was a cool look. The Kiowa pulled back his lance, waved it once over his head, and then wheeled his horse and galloped off.

"Sky Eyes *muy bravo*," Laughing Boy said when the Kiowa had gone. He seemed pleased. "Takes-Many-Scalps does not like."

"That's a joke," Sul said under his breath. "Takes-Many-Scalps hates me." To Laughing Boy he said, "I can see that. Did he say why?"

"Kiowa do not like white men. He says you are bad medicine." The young warrior seemed to grin at the idea. "Mount your horse. We go to the village now — be there by sundown."

Sul nodded and, grasping a hank of mane, swung himself onto the back of the extra horse. "And if Takes-Many-Scalps is there, I'd better stay out of his way," he told himself.

As they rode on, he risked a quick look over one shoulder just in case, but saw nothing. If Hanse was on their back trail, he more than likely wouldn't let himself be seen. "And if he isn't, I'll tell the chief who he is and ask to be freed. If they won't let me go," Sul vowed, "I'll get away somehow and go back home. But Hanse will come after me. I know he will."

They came in view of the Comanche camp about two hours before sunset and halted to speak to a couple of mounted lookouts. While one of them rode on to the camp, Laughing Boy and Tall Horse repainted their faces and displayed the Kickapoo scalps they had taken. Then their party again rode on.

Although he was tired and hungry, Sul straightened proudly
on the back of the extra horse. He looked eagerly around, not
wanting to miss anything, and was surprised by the size of the
camp. More than forty tepees straggled along the banks of a
nearby stream while smoke spiraled upwards from numerous fires
where women were cooking the evening meal. Here and there
children played among the tepees. Even from this distance he
could hear their laughter and the barking of the camp dogs.

As the rider who had galloped on ahead neared the camp, he
began yelling. Soon the whole camp was in an uproar as the
Comanches poured out of their tepees, singing and dancing.
Laughing Boy smiled with satisfaction at these sounds of welcome.
"Now we go in," he said to Sul and urged his mount forward.

The boy was aware of many eyes on him as Comanche men,
women, and children crowded around the two warriors and their
captive. Some of the Comanches pointed at him and said something to their friends. Sul was sure they were talking about him
and tried to keep from blushing. Several young girls laughed at
him, while others stared. One old woman even put out a hand
and touched his knee as he rode by.

Accompanied by the crowd, Laughing Boy and Tall Horse
walked their horses between two tepees and headed for the center of the camp, Sul following. The boy tried not to stare at the
laughing, shouting throng swarming around him, but he was too
curious to keep his eyes off the Comanches for long. "Do I look
as strange to them as they do to me?" he wondered, eyeing their
clothing and ornaments.

Unexpectedly the crowd parted, and a figure in white man's
clothes but with long hair braided like a Comanche's strode forward. As Sul rode past, the man grabbed the rope bridle of the
horse the boy was riding and jerked it to a stop. "Get down,
boy!" he ordered harshly.

AT THE VILLAGE OF THE PEOPLE

S ul hesitated, wondering what would happen next. Before Laughing Boy or Tall Horse could react, the stranger grabbed the boy by the right arm and pulled him from the horse. Sul flinched, but the stranger ignored his pain.

Shoving the boy behind him as if to protect him, the man began shouting in Comanche at Laughing Boy and Tall Horse. Words peppered the pair like hailstones, but to Sul's surprise Laughing Boy didn't answer back. At last the young warrior shrugged, threw down the boy's boots, and rode on with Tall Horse — without their captive. The rest of the crowd flowed off after them, leaving Sul standing behind his rescuer.

"Young fools," the man growled, stooping to pick up the boots, "breaking the '46 treaty like that." He turned to face Sul. "Who are you, boy, and what are you doing here?" he asked roughly. As an afterthought, he added, "I don't know if you've heard of me, but I'm Dr. Sturm."

Sul relaxed and grinned. Dr. Sturm, who lived with the Comanches, was well known as a friend of both red and white. "I'm Sul Ross, sir, and I have heard of you. My father met you several years ago."

"Not one of Shap Ross' boys?" the physician asked, more kindly now, and Sul nodded. "But what are you doing out here? Laughing Boy hasn't raided the settlements, has he?"

"It's a long story, sir," Sul began. Then his nostrils twitched. Somewhere nearby meat was being grilled, and the delicious smell made him suddenly weak with hunger. Hoping he didn't look as hungry as he felt, he started to continue with his tale but Sturm cut him off short.

"Then it can wait until you've had something to eat." The doctor handed back the boots and noticed that Sul grimaced as he took them. "What's wrong with your arm?"

"A Kickapoo arrow," Sul replied.

"More story," Sturm smiled. "But first things first. Come with me to the lodge of my host, White Bull. His wife is old, but she's still the best cook in camp."

Sul grinned again. "That sounds good. My stomach and backbone are beginning to rub together."

Dr. Sturm waited until Sul had finished eating and had used sign language to thank the elderly Comanche who was his host before examining the arrow wound on the boy's arm.

"This is healing," the physician said, redressing the injury with some ointment he kept among his things in White Bull's tepee. "Just keep it as clean and dry as possible the next few days. Who treated it for you, anyway?" he went on. "Whoever did it knew what they were doing."

Sul knew it was time to reveal Hanse's identity. "I am the *tua* of He-Who-Sees-Far, the white son of Gray Wolf," he said as Mason had told him. "He treated us both after our fight with the Kickapoos, although his wound was more serious than mine. That is how Laughing Boy and Tall Horse captured me. Hanse was sleeping at the time — he'd lost a lot of blood."

Dr. Sturm gave a low whistle. "Those two stole you from Gray Wolf's white son?" he repeated. "Did they know it at the time?"

"Hanse called himself 'Far Eyes,' but they didn't seem to know the name," Sul explained. "He said if I was ever around older Comanches they would know who he was."

Dr. Sturm laughed. "Yes, they would," he agreed. "Do you know who Gray Wolf was?" When Sul shook his head, the man answered his own question. "He was one of the most feared medicine men this band of Comanches ever had. And He-Who-Sees-Far is still remembered by the People. Even if your friend doesn't trace you here, you won't have any trouble getting back to Waco. Chief Ketumse's people will be glad to send you home when they hear you're under the protection of Gray Wolf's foster son."

Sul grinned at this news. "Do you think I can get my knife and revolver back? He-Who-Sees-Far gave them to me."

"I'll get them for you," Sturm promised. "It will be better not to go to Chief Ketumse tonight — he's got the brother of another chief and three Seminoles who came into camp today as his guests — but I'll take your case to him in the morning. In the meantime, White Bull extends the hospitality of his lodge."

"Tell White Bull I thank him," Sul said. Then, remembering what Mason had told him about the Seminoles, he asked, "What are the Seminoles doing here?"

Dr. Sturm looked surprised by his question. "Their business is with the chief," he explained. "If it is important, he will tell the rest of us at council in the morning."

Sul started to say something more, but before he could go on, the flap covering the door of the tepee flipped open. An Indian boy about his own age burst in, speaking excitedly. When the youngster noticed their visitor, he broke off and sat quietly down on the other side of Dr. Sturm.

"Sul Ross, this is my foster son, Runs Fast," the doctor said in introduction.

Sul started making the signs for greeting and friendship, but Sturm cut him off short. "Runs Fast speaks English," he said. The doctor turned to his adopted son. "Yes, Sul is the sky-eyed one you heard about in the camp," he said. "He is the *tua* of He-Who-Sees-Far, the white son of Gray Wolf."

"You are son of He-Who-Sees-Far?" Runs Fast asked earnestly.

"No — I am his *tua*." Wondering why Runs Fast had misunderstood, Sul looked questioningly at Dr. Sturm.

"*Tua* means 'son' or 'brother's son' — what you'd call nephew," the physician explained.

Sul nodded. "Then He-Who-Sees-Far is my almost uncle," he told the other boy with a grin. "He and my father have been friends for a long time."

Runs Fast regarded him gravely. "Who then is the father of Sky Eyes?" he asked.

"Do you remember the tall man from the Brazos who visited our camp two years ago?" Dr. Sturm asked his son. "He is the father of Sky Eyes."

Sul felt the Indian boy studying him and blushed. Finally Runs Fast nodded. "Your father is plenty tall, plenty brave," he said. "He has sky eyes too."

"Pa is very tall," Sul answered. "I'll probably never be as tall as he is."

"No matter if you are as brave," Runs Fast answered. "Where is He-Who-Sees-Far?"

"He will come," Sul said. "You will see him soon."

"Soon enough," Dr. Sturm agreed. He smiled at Sul. "From what you've told me, boy, you've had a busy couple of days. Now is the time for sleep."

Runs Fast took the hint and stood. "Come, Sky Eyes. I will show you where you can sleep."

Sometime later, Sul lay on his back on the buffalo robe which had been spread for him near Runs Fast's pallet. After the heat of the day, it was cool in the tepee. The sides of the lodge had been rolled up so that the evening breeze could blow through, and he was glad for the blanket White Bull's wife had loaned him. Although he was very tired, he couldn't sleep. Somewhere in the camp he could hear the throb of drums and the whoops and yells of the Comanches celebrating their victory over the Kickapoos. It was a scalp dance, Dr. Sturm had said.

"I'm glad Hanse is so respected for being the adopted son of Gray Wolf," the boy told himself. "And thanks to Pa and Dr. Sturm, I'm being treated like a guest and not a captive." For a while he pondered what would have been his fate if his father hadn't taught him how to act around Indians or if Dr. Sturm hadn't rescued him or if Hanse hadn't been He-Who-Sees-Far.

Sul's thoughts raced. If the Seminoles succeeded in uniting the other tribes for war on the frontier, soon the Comanches might be celebrating the taking of Texan scalps. And Texas children would possibly be captives in the villages of the People. Suddenly the boy felt it was no longer exciting but instead rather alarming to be a guest in a Comanche village. "I hope Hanse gets here soon," he said to himself, turning over to pillow his head on his arms.

When Sul awakened the next morning, he found he was the only one in the tepee except for Runs Fast who was sitting nearby. "Where is everybody?" he asked with a yawn.

"White Bull and my father go see chief," the Indian boy answered. "White Bull's wife outside cooking. Food be ready soon."

"Good," Sul said, rolling over and sitting up. "I'm hungry."

Runs Fast eyed him uncertainly. "You swim, Sky Eyes?"

"Whenever I get the chance," Sul answered. The thought of a swim made him suddenly aware of the dirty clothes he'd worn since leaving Waco. "I'm sorry about how I look," he told Runs Fast, "but I don't have anything better to put on."

"If you stay with us, White Bull's wife will make you new clothes," the Indian boy said politely. "Right now, come with me."

Sul went with Runs Fast. The Indian boy again took him to a place away from camp where he could relieve himself and then to the stream where he could wash. Belatedly remembering his arrow wound, Sul did not go in for a swim but rather used his bandana to wash his hands and face and his silk neckerchief to dry them.

Runs Fast pointed as he retied the neckerchief around his neck. "That is like your eyes," the Indian boy said admiringly.

Remembering what his father had said about the importance of giving Indians presents, Sul untied the neckerchief and held it out. "Take it as a gift in honor of our friendship," he said.

Runs Fast took the silk eagerly. "I thank you, Sky Eyes," he replied. "You ready? We go back now."

Sul grinned and tied his wet bandana about his neck. "I'm more than ready," he said. "I've been hungry since I woke up."

"Could we go look at the camp?" Sul asked when they had finished eating.

Runs Fast shook his head emphatically. "My father says stay here with me until chief talks to you." He held up a bow and a quiver of arrows. "Later we will go shoot," he said.

"I'd like that," Sul agreed. He spent a quiet morning with Runs Fast, watching White Bull make arrows and his wife scrape a buffalo hide she had staked to the ground. He was glad when Dr. Sturm returned just before mid-day and told him to get ready to go to Chief Ketumse's lodge.

"I've told the chief your story," the doctor said, as the two of them walked across the camp later, "but he'll want to question you himself. Although he speaks some English, he wants me to translate for him into Comanche so the other elders can understand. Stand respectfully and wait quietly until the chief speaks to you."

The boy nodded. He wanted to ask, "Laughing Boy and Tall Horse won't get into trouble, will they?" but saw they were approaching the circle of elders and warriors and so did not speak. While the chief sat in the place of honor, Laughing Boy and Tall Horse had taken their places among several younger warriors at the side. They did not look at Sul. Across from them, and by himself, sat the Kiowa, Takes-Many-Scalps. He made no secret of glaring hatefully at the boy. Near the chief sat three warriors in Indian costume Sul had never seen before; he guessed they were the visiting Seminoles.

Chief Ketumse motioned Sul forward with Dr. Sturm. As the boy followed the physician, he could see that the Comanche cradled a ceremonial pipe across his knees. Before the chief could speak, another uproar arose from the edge of the camp. Sul could hear shouting. The chief kept his calm expression, but he made signs that Sturm and the boy were to sit down at one side and to the rear of the group.

Sul looked a question at the physician as they did so. "A blue-coat soldier is riding into the camp," Sturm answered.

"Hanse!" Sul started to stand up, but Sturm shook his head.

"He will have more honor if you sit quietly," the doctor warned, and the boy sank back down. "Remember," Sturm said, "these men have been told that you are his *tua*."

Sul ducked his head in agreement. Steeling himself to show no emotion, he sat back to watch for the sergeant's appearance. Finally Mason came riding up on Chief, leading Saber with an antelope slung over the roan's saddle. Just outside the circle, he halted the horses and deliberately dismounted. His fierce eyes scanned those sitting around; Sul felt sure that Hanse spotted him there next to Dr. Sturm, but Mason's expression didn't change. He made the friendship sign and spoke to the chief and assembled elders and warriors in Comanche.

"He says he is Gray Wolf's white son, He-Who-Sees-Far, and he has come for his *tua* who was stolen from him," the doctor translated for Sul's benefit, but the translation wasn't necessary. The boy could tell by the way the Comanches gave Mason their whole attention that Hanse had revealed his identity.

Chief Ketumse spoke then, and again Dr. Sturm translated.

"He says the white son of Gray Wolf is welcome, and that the *tua* of He-Who-Sees-Far is safe in the lodges of the People."

Mason spoke again, this time more forcefully. Beside Sul, Dr. Sturm repeated what he had said. "He says his honor has been shamed by the theft of his *tua*, and he wants damages — five horses, fifteen buffalo robes, and dried meat for two men."

Sul gaped at this demand. "Damages?" he whispered. "Why?"

"Custom," the doctor explained. "Any time one Comanche injures another, the injured party has a right to demand and receive damages — if he's powerful enough. And I'd say your friend is plenty powerful."

Evidently the Comanches agreed, for most of them nodded. Chief Ketumse spoke to Laughing Boy and Tall Horse, who likewise agreed. Then he turned back to speak to Hanse.

"It is agreed," Sturm translated once more. "The damages will be paid."

With a yell, Takes-Many-Scalps leaped to his feet. Waving his arms angrily, the warrior began shouting. Sturm spoke quietly to Sul. "You shouldn't need a translator for that. As far as the Kiowa is concerned, the answer is 'No!' And he says that rather than let a white man so rob the People, he will fight and kill him himself!"

HE-WHO-SEES-FAR

"**N**o! Hanse can't fight him!" Sul told Dr. Sturm wildly. "He took a Kickapoo arrow in the shoulder when I was hit. It can't be healed already. Takes-Many-Scalps will kill him!"

Sturm laid a hand on the boy's arm. "Your friend knows the customs of the People. He wouldn't make a bid for damages if he wasn't ready to fight for them."

Sul calmed down then, for he saw Mason frowning at him.

With a long, steady look at the boy, the sergeant turned slowly to face the Kiowa. He said something in Comanche, making Takes-Many-Scalps gabble with fury, but the Kiowa made no move. Someone in the group laughed but immediately smothered the outburst. Most of the other men looked gravely disapproving, as if they were affronted by the warrior's anger.

"He says the Kiowa dogs have long barked around the lodges of the People," Dr. Sturm translated. "Rightly are they named 'Rascal.'"

Sul relaxed a little. "I thought the others didn't like the Kiowa. Is he really unpopular?"

"He's about as welcome in this village as the smallpox," Dr. Sturm replied.

Sul started to ask why, but Hanse was speaking again, this time to Chief Ketumse. The boy leaned forward, concentrating on what was going on. The Comanche held out the ceremonial pipe and the sergeant stepped forward to take it. Holding the pipe at arm's length, he offered it first to the sky, next to the ground, and then to the four directions. Sul started to ask what was happening, but the solemn expressions around him made him hold his tongue. When Mason at last put the pipe to his lips, he gave six short puffs in the same directions before handing the object back to the chief and speaking again.

"He's taking a serious oath," Dr. Sturm explained in a low whisper. "He is calling upon the sun and the earth and the sky powers to witness that what he says is the truth."

Sul nodded, glad now he had not spoken during that part of the ceremony.

The physician went on, translating as the sergeant spoke. "He's reminding them that he is He-Who-Sees-Far and of the winter of the big snows."

"What does that mean?" Sul whispered back.

"I don't know," Sturm replied, "but some of these men remember. Look at them."

Sul glanced around at the Comanche elders and warriors. As the physician had pointed out, some of the older Comanches were showing signs of growing excitement. Several of them spoke together and nodded. "They're agreeing," he said joyfully.

"They're agreeing to the truth of his oath," Dr. Sturm said.

"What's Hanse saying now?" Sul asked as Mason spoke again. Here and there, a warrior stirred uneasily. Sul noticed at the same time that Runs Fast had come to sit behind them.

"He said he didn't realize that a rascal could change the customs of the People, but since the warriors of this village were now women he would fight the Kiowa himself," Dr. Sturm explained. "He says he will have to make his medicine first, though."

Even as Sturm spoke, Hanse put back his head and howled like a wolf. Sul jumped, the howl was so real. Several of the younger warriors did too. The elders, however, leaned closer, their eyes gleaming expectantly as Mason began to pace and stamp, chanting all the while. Before he could move around the circle, three warriors — Laughing Boy, Tall Horse, and another — jumped to their feet and went to stand by the sergeant.

"Now what?" Sul asked fearfully as the Comanches began speaking.

Dr. Sturm laughed. "Don't worry — they're on his side now. Takes-Many-Scalps won't make any more trouble. He'll have those four to answer to if he does."

"But what did Hanse do?"

"Challenged their courage — something they couldn't stand. And they didn't want him finishing the curse he'd started putting on them. Ketumse's people still have enough respect for Gray Wolf's memory that they didn't want that." Sturm pointed to Takes-Many-Scalps. "Look — he's backing down!" As the physician spoke, the Kiowa turned and stalked from the council.

Sul watched him go before turning back to what was going on in the council. Chief Ketumse had just finished speaking to Hanse, and Mason had answered him once more. Dr. Sturm took the boy's arm.

"Go back with Runs Fast to White Bull's tepee," he said. "The chief has insisted that your friend stay and take part in the council so it will be a while yet before he can join you." The doctor smiled consolingly. "Right now, you're not very important, you know. You're only a boy and there are men — warriors — for the chief to deal with."

Sul got to his feet. "I didn't think I was," he said.

"It is good what He-Who-Sees-Far said about the Kiowa," Runs Fast told Sul as they left the council. "He *is* a rascal."

"Your father said the others don't like him," Sul agreed. "What has he done?"

Runs Fast stopped and turned to face the other boy. "He shamed my grandfather — ran off with Grandfather's youngest wife."

"Wouldn't Takes-Many-Scalps pay damages?" Sul asked.

Runs Fast snorted. "He is a fierce warrior — we could not make him pay. I wish He-Who-Sees-Far would fight and kill him."

"I'm glad Hanse didn't have to," Sul answered. "He was wounded in our fight with the Kickapoos."

Runs Fast looked at him with increased respect. "You fought Kickapoos? Take any scalps?" he added eagerly.

Sul shook his head. "I shot one, though."

"You *muy afortunado*," Runs Fast said, turning and walking on. "Wish I was with you."

Sul followed. "Do you know the story of the winter of the big snows?" he asked his new friend curiously. "Hanse never told me about that."

It was Runs Fast's turn to shake his head. "White Bull will know. When he returns we ask him."

Later Sul sat cross-legged in the shade cast by White Bull's tepee with Runs Fast and listened as the old man told the requested story. By then Dr. Sturm had returned and also joined them. Nearby White Bull's wife continued her work on the buffalo hide she was tanning.

"Many winters ago much snow fell," Sturm translated for the boy. "It came early and stayed late and snowed many times in between. Spring came late so food began to run short in the village. Day after day our hunters went out but found no prey. Twice Gray Wolf made buffalo dance medicine, but no buffalo were to be found. Soon there was talk we would have to kill and eat our horses just to stay alive."

The old man paused before continuing. Sul leaned forward, listening even more intently as the physician went on.

"Then one morning, Little Wild Cat, the white son of Gray Wolf, came to his foster father. He was little boy then, younger than you. 'Father,' he said, 'I see many buffalo.' Then Gray Wolf asked him where and Little Wild Cat said, 'Near flat mountain.'"

"Comanche Peak?" Sul asked eagerly.

When Dr. Sturm relayed this question, White Bull agreed. Smiling at the boys, he went on with his story. "We sent our best hunters. Near flat mountain they found buffalo as Gray Wolf's white son had said. They killed many, and our village had meat to last to spring. It is then Gray Wolf gave his white son a new name, He-Who-Sees-Far."

"So that's how Hanse got the nickname 'Far Eyes,'" Sul said. "But how did he know the buffalo were there?"

"Why don't you ask him yourself," Sturm replied, pointing. "Here he comes."

Hiding his excitement, Sul got to his feet and stood quietly waiting as Mason rode up leading Saber. The sergeant dismounted to greet White Bull and Dr. Sturm. Only when these formalities were over and White Bull's wife had come to lead away the horses, did the sergeant turn his attention to the boy.

"You all right, Sully?" he asked, putting a hand on Sul's shoulder. "I couldn't get here until now."

"I've been well treated," Sul answered. "Dr. Sturm, White Bull, and Runs Fast have seen to that." He beamed up at his friend. "Thanks for coming after me. I knew you would." His thanks said, he hurried on with the news he had discovered. "Hanse, there are Seminoles in camp. They've been meeting with Chief Ketumse."

"I saw 'em. That's one reason I wasn't in any hurry to leave the council. There's a couple of Anadarkos here too. Maybe I can talk to 'em before we leave an' save us a trip to José María's village."

"I'm glad you saw them," Sul said. He paused before asking the question which had been bothering him. "You didn't think I had broken my parole, did you?"

"Young'un, when I first woke up an' found you gone, I didn't know what to think," Mason told him. "Then I saw your horse an' rifle still in camp, an' I knew you hadn't run away. When I went lookin' for you an' spotted them Comanche moccasin prints mixed in with your boot prints, I figured Laughin' Boy had come after us an' grabbed you." The sergeant sat down on the buffalo robe beside Dr. Sturm and looked up at the boy. "I hope you put up a good fight."

Sul started to tell Hanse what had really happened but then remembered that he shouldn't boast. "Ask Tall Horse or Laughing Boy," he said, likewise sitting down. "They'll tell you."

Mason's eyes glowed in approval. "Figured you had when I found the place where you'd hit the ground. What'd they do — clout you one?"

Sul nodded. "I tried calling you, but they shut me up."

"Were you afraid?" Mason continued.

Sul frowned at this probing. "No, not really. Not until we met the Kiowa, and then I tried not to show it. But why do you want to know, Hanse?" He blushed. "Is it because you think I've been bragging? I've tried hard not to."

Mason gave Sul one of his rare smiles. "I have a report to make," he said. "An' I wanted to be sure of my facts."

Sul grinned in understanding. So Hanse would tell Pa — and others — how he had handled himself. "How did you find me so quickly?" he asked to change the subject.

"I knew the campin' places west of Comanche Peak," Mason explained. "This here's a good spot, an' Ketumse's band has used it on an' off for years. It wasn't hard to find even though I lost your trail at one place."

"Did you find my belt in that creek bed?" Sul asked. "I dropped it off to try to mark the trail."

"Just where you left it," Mason agreed. "It's on my saddle now."

Sul's eyes sparkled. "I hoped you would," he said, clasping his hands around one knee. "How did you know the buffalo were here the winter of the big snows?" he asked suddenly. When the sergeant looked surprised at his question the boy added, "White Bull told us the story."

"I don't know if it was a dream or somethin' like a vision," Mason said. "I was young — maybe all of seven that winter. What I do remember is that I 'saw' them buffalo an' told Gray Wolf. Since then I've known some other things before they happened, like when Greta an' our girls died. I felt somethin' was wrong an' came back to find 'em all dead an' buried."

Sul looked at his friend in wonder. Before he could ask, "How does it work?" Runs Fast spoke up.

"Is it part of your medicine?" the Indian boy asked.

"It ain't got anythin' to do with magic," Mason told him.

Surprisingly, Dr. Sturm provided an answer of sorts. "The Scots and Irish call it 'second sight'," he said. "And it's not uncommon among the Indian tribes, too. No wonder Gray Wolf and the others recognized the ability."

"Do you have to do anything to make it work?" Sul asked, awed.

Mason shook his head. "Not a thing. An' it don't work all the time," he admitted. "There've been times when I could have used it — like the other day." He smiled again briefly at the boy. "But I would have come after you, young'un, no matter how long the trail."

"I know you would have, Hanse," Sul answered. The boy looked up. "Here come Laughing Boy and Tall Horse," he said.

"An' their wives leadin' the packhorses," the sergeant added, standing back up. "Be on your dignity, young'un. It won't do to offend any of 'em now that they're payin' for runnin' off with you."

Sul sat up straight and tall as the young warriors approached, wearing their finery. Behind them, young women led five laden packhorses.

"Looks like they've brought everythin'," Mason said, turning to greet their visitors in Comanche.

Sul watched interestedly as the conversation continued. Laughing Boy and Tall Horse did not so much as look his way, though, even when they gave Hanse his knife and Colt. When Laughing Boy handed over the revolver, he seemed to do so with great reluctance. At last the two young warriors and their wives departed, leaving the packhorses behind.

"They wouldn't even look at me," Sul said sadly. "And I wanted to say good-bye."

"They've got to save face before their people, young'un," Mason told the boy as he handed over his weapons. "You'll probably see 'em again tonight. It'd be bad manners for us to rush off before the feastin' an' dancin' to be held this evenin', especially since I'm one of the guests of honor."

"I'm glad they're honoring you," Sul said. "Could we go around and look at the camp? I haven't seen much of it yet."

Mason yawned and stretched. "I've been on the trail since I woke up an' found you missin'. Let me get a couple hours' sleep, an' I'll take you anywhere you want to go, young'un."

"Catch up on your sleep, Sergeant," Dr. Sturm said. "My son and I would be honored to introduce the *tua* of He-Who-Sees-Far to the life of the People."

Sul blushed. "I'd like to do that," he said carefully, not wanting to be impolite, "but Hanse is supposed to be my uncle. If you don't mind, I'd rather wait and go around the camp with him."

Dr. Sturm smiled in understanding. "Let's compromise," he said. "We will entertain you here until your 'uncle' wakes up. Then you can go with him wherever you like."

Sul beamed at this suggestion. "Thanks, Dr. Sturm. I'd really like that." He looked at Mason. "That would be all right, won't it, Hanse?"

The sergeant nodded. "That's a good idea, young'un, only you'd better get some shut-eye between now an' sundown. Them dances usually last all night an' you'll be wantin' sleep before mornin'."

"I will," Sul promised.

KNIFE IN THE DARK

Sul spent a happy afternoon with Runs Fast and Dr. Sturm, learning to shoot the Indian boy's bow and, during the heat of the day, napping for a short time. Later he visited with White Bull as the old warrior exhibited his shield, arrows, and bow and then answered Sul's questions about how his weapons were made.

As the afternoon wore on, White Bull told the boys stories of Comanche life and folklore of the People. One of these tales was about the Great-Owl-That-Eats-Men, a gigantic bird which once lived in Texas.

"How could an owl be that big?" Sul wanted to know.

"Don't know," was White Bull's answer through Dr. Sturm, "but I see tracks in river bed near here when I little boy. This big." The old man's hands showed a measurement more than a foot across. "When I asked what make them, my grandfather said Great-Owl-That-Eats-Men."

In spite of himself, Sul felt a little shiver of fear. In school he had read about the bones of great beasts which had been uncovered from the earth, so it was possible that once a giant owl had swooped over this part of Texas.

"Where is the giant owl now?" he asked White Bull. Looking at Runs Fast, Sul was surprised to see his Indian friend squirm uneasily at his question as if he, too, felt some fear.

In a cave in mountains across big river," was the old man's reply.

Sul relaxed. "That's a long way from here," he said and turned to Runs Fast. "Would you like to look for it someday?" he asked his friend. The Comanche boy shook his head vigorously.

"Look for what, young'un?" Mason asked, rising from where he had been sleeping and coming to join them.

Sul grinned at the sergeant. "The giant owl — the one that eats people. White Bull has just been telling us about it. Have you ever heard the stories, Hanse?"

Mason nodded at Runs Fast as he sat down. "Those of us who were raised by the People have heard a lot of stories about the Great-Owl-That-Eats-Men," he told Sul. "When I was little, my foster mother used to scare me with 'em all the time." He smiled slightly at the boy. "You ready to go look at the camp?"

"I want to see as much as I can while I'm here," Sul said eagerly. "Where do you think we should start?"

"Let's get our horses an' ride around," Mason suggested.

Sul sighed contentedly as he settled into Saber's saddle a few minutes later. It was good to be on his own horse once more.

"Happy, young'un?" Mason asked, mounting and feeling for his stirrup with his boot toe.

Sul grinned broadly. "That Kickapoo horse Laughing Boy made me ride was so hard-gaited it jarred my teeth. Saber's a dream after that."

"So your pa made a good choice when he bought him for you," the sergeant pointed out.

"Pa really knows horses," Sul admitted, "but that doesn't mean I want to live with him!"

Mason ignored his outburst. "Let's ride," he said, wheeling his sorrel.

Sul looked around as they started off through the camp. "Where are all the horses?" he asked to change the subject. "I thought the Comanches owned horses, but so far all I've seen are a few picketed among the tepees."

"They do, young'un," Mason told him. "A camp this size will have a pony herd of four or five hundred head. Those you see here are only their owners' favorites — their best war ponies an' ridin' horses. The others are out with the herd."

"Five hundred?" Sul echoed. "Hanse, there aren't that many horses in Waco, and it's a lot bigger than this camp. Why so many?"

"Horses mean wealth to a Comanche, young'un. An' stealin' 'em is a game, a way of provin' courage. They start out young, doin' it as boys, an' keep at it."

Sul wanted to ask if Hanse had also stolen horses as a boy, but before he could speak the sergeant went on.

"The herd guards have got this camp's ponies some place nearby where the grass an' water are good," Mason explained. "They'd bring 'em up mighty fast if the camp came under attack."

Just then they passed a lodge on the outskirts of the camp. Sul glanced that way as they rode by and saw Takes-Many-Scalps step out. The Kiowa glared hatefully at them before ducking back into the tepee, his hand on his knife. "He would kill us if he got the chance," Sul told himself.

The next few hours passed quickly. True to his promise, Mason took the boy all over the camp, explaining the customs of the People and telling some of his experiences while living with them. The Comanches, however, seemed to ignore their presence.

"They're bein' polite," Mason explained when Sul asked about their hosts' lack of interest. "Gray Wolf might've passed his power on to me, an' they ain't takin' any chances."

"Did he?" Sul asked, remembering that wolf howl Hanse had made which had caused him to jump.

"Only his healin' lore," the sergeant said. "Once in a while what medicine — magic — I did pick up from him has come in handy — like this mornin'. I guess real learnin' ain't ever wasted."

"That's why I want more," Sul told his friend.

At another place in camp, they halted to watch several women setting up the poles for a tepee. Working together, the women then lifted the buffalo skin cover into place.

"How will they get the cover fastened at the top?" Sul wanted to know. "It's a long way from the ground."

"Watch," Mason said. As he spoke, two of the women climbed upon the shoulders of two others. They began fastening the cover while a third pinned the hides in place down the front. In only a few minutes the lodge stood ready for use.

"That was quick," Sul said when the women had finished.

Mason nodded. "It's even quicker to take one down," he answered, moving his horse forward. "This whole camp could be ready to move in about twenty minutes. That's why the Comanches are so hard to catch when they do make a raid. They strike quick an' hit hard, an' then even their villages are gone when the Dragoons come after 'em."

"I hope war doesn't break out," Sul said, heeling Saber into a walk beside the sorrel. "Runs Fast is my friend — I'd hate to think of us being on different sides."

"That's why we've got to keep the peace as long as possible," Mason told him. "There're good people on both sides of the frontier who are goin' to be caught in the middle if an Indian war breaks out. I don't want to see that happen."

Sul frowned worriedly. "What if the Dragoons had to fight this band of Comanches — Laughing Boy or Tall Horse or even the old men who knew Gray Wolf?"

Mason's expression did not change. "Then I'd do my duty, young'un, no matter what — like a good soldier." He gestured widely to take in the camp around them. "My loyalty ain't to the Comanches any more — it's to my own people. An' yours should be too," he added meaningfully, glancing sharply at the boy.

Sul felt his face burn and dropped his gaze. He had been too busy enjoying his adventure to worry about Mason's opinion of his running away, but now he realized he had to face it. "Hanse thinks I'm shirking my duty by not being at home to help Ma and Pa," he told himself guiltily. Then he added, "I'd rather take five lickings from Pa over it than have Hanse bawl me out."

With another blush, Sul recalled his first buffalo hunt the year before. He had fired too soon, scaring off the herd and ruining everyone else's hunting. Pa had given him a hiding on the spot for disobedience of orders, but far worse had been the choice few words spoken on the subject by Hanse. Sul had never before felt so ashamed, and the blistering words — describing the way he had let everyone down — remained burned into his memory. And now . . . fearing that the sergeant was going to give him another tongue-lashing, the boy looked up, wretchedly, into his friend's face.

He found Mason watching him closely. But instead of beginning a dressing-down, the sergeant indicated the late afternoon sun. "We'd better get back to White Bull's tepee," he said casually. "The celebration will be startin' soon, an' we need to get ready."

Relieved, Sul sighed and relaxed. "That's fine with me," he said.

"I've been invited to sit with the chiefs," Mason told Sul as he and the boy later walked with Dr. Sturm and Runs Fast to the place where the feasting and dancing were to be held. "Comanche young'uns can join in the feastin', but they're expected to stay in the background while men an' women do the dancin'. Stick with Runs Fast an' you won't get into trouble."

"All right, Hanse, I will," Sul agreed. Curiously he looked

around. The celebration was to be held in a cleared area. A large fire had been built in the center, and buffalo robes had been spread for the guests of honor. At the edge of the circle were gathered those who had come for the feasting. Already women were serving the guests, the men first and then the boys. Sul took a seat on a blanket with Runs Fast behind the men; soon a woman brought them both helpings of parched corn and antelope stew in wooden bowls.

"When does the dancing begin?" he asked the Comanche boy when they had finished their supper.

"Soon," Runs Fast replied. "We wait now for the sun to go down. It is cooler then."

Sul nodded. He had left his hat and revolver in the tepee, and already the evening breeze was ruffling his curls. "I just didn't want to miss anything," he said.

As he spoke, a group of older men carrying drums arrived and took their seats at one side. When the sun went down, these men began beating their drums and singing. The dance had begun.

At first Sul found the dancing fascinating, especially the actions of the whip leader who had the right to demand that anyone dance when he pointed his whip at them.

"Even greatest warriors dance when he says so," Runs Fast told him. "Only way they can stop is tell their bravest deed."

Fascinating as this was, as the evening wore on and one dance blended into another, Sul lost interest in the dancing and began watching the dancers and spectators themselves. Among those viewing the festivities were the three visiting Seminoles and the Kiowa, Takes-Many-Scalps, who sat apart from their Comanche hosts. During one dance the four of them sat down together across the fire from where Sul and Runs Fast sat and began speaking among themselves. Soon a Comanche warrior joined them.

"Look at that," Sul said to Runs Fast. "The Kiowa is sure getting friendly with those Seminoles."

Runs Fast looked where he pointed. "That is not good," the Indian boy agreed. "My father says they speak too much of war."

"He-Who-Sees-Far says it means trouble for both our peoples," Sul said. "Who is that warrior who just joined them?" he asked. "He walks like a chief."

"That is Buffalo Hump's brother," Runs Fast told him. "His band desires war, and he speaks against Chief Ketumse in the council."

Sul stared at the warriors. "I wish they were using sign language so we could know what they are saying," he said. He looked up to see if Hanse had noticed the little group, but Mason was busy talking to a couple of Comanche elders.

Beside him, Runs Fast grinned. "They speak the language of the People," he told his friend.

"But they're Seminoles," Sul protested. "Why should they speak Comanche?"

"Many tribes speak our language," Runs Fast said proudly. "You shoot Kickapoo, I listen to Seminoles," he added, starting to rise. "Like counting coup on enemy . . . much honor in danger."

"No," Sul said, "if there is danger we'll both go."

Runs Fast chuckled. "You are brave, Sky Eyes, but you look too much like a white man."

"I can fix that," Sul said. Turning his back to the fire, the boy pulled his shirt off over his head and tied it around his waist over his britches so that it looked like he was wearing a breechclout and leggings like Runs Fast. Untying his bandana, he retied it around his curls like a headband. "Now how do I look?" he asked, swinging back to face his friend.

Runs Fast laughed again, but this time he nodded his approval. "More like the People. In dark be hard to tell that you are white."

Leaving their place with the other spectators, the boys dropped back from the fire and walked around the tepees to come up behind the Seminoles and the others in the darkness.

"We must go like snakes from here," Runs Fast said softly in Sul's ear. He eased himself onto his stomach and began wriggling noiselessly forward.

Sul followed, moving as quietly as he could. From somewhere ahead of them he could hear low, fierce voices. The two boys moved forward about twenty feet before Runs Fast turned and gripped Sul's wrist in warning.

The boy stopped his creeping and lay still beside Runs Fast. About ten feet ahead, he could see the backs of the Seminoles and another warrior. For several minutes the Indian boy remained motionless, listening intently; then he tapped Sul on the arm and pointed back the way they had come.

Sul nodded and began inching backwards, followed by Runs Fast. It took them some time to retreat from their observation post, but at last they reached the safety of a nearby tepee.

"What did you find out?" Sul whispered as they sat down near a picketed pony on the far side of the lodge.

"The Seminoles urge war on your people," Runs Fast answered in a low voice. "Buffalo Hump seeks scalps and horses too."

Sul remembered Takes-Many-Scalps. "And the Kiowa?" he asked.

Runs Fast was puzzled. "It strange — he was not there."

"He was when we left the fire just a few minutes ago," Sul said, looking around. "Do you think he might have spot — "

With a yell, Takes-Many-Scalps leaped out from behind the tepee and lunged at them. Sul saw the distant firelight gleam on a knife blade as the Kiowa raised one arm over his head.

Runs Fast sprang to his feet. "Run!" he yelled.

Sul jumped up too. His boot soles slipped in the grass, and he stumbled, one hand brushing the ground, and almost fell. He felt the wind of a near miss as the Kiowa slashed at him with the knife. Somehow he recovered his balance and sprinted after Runs Fast. Takes-Many-Scalps shouted and dashed after them.

"It's easy to see how Runs Fast got his name," Sul told himself as they darted away ahead of the Kiowa. "I only hope Takes-Many-Scalps isn't a fast runner too." Racing after the other boy, he tried to follow as closely as possible on his Indian friend's heels as they dodged back into the camp.

As they ran, it seemed to Sul that he could feel Takes-Many-Scalps breathing down his neck. Thinking of the knife in the Kiowa's hand, he decided he didn't want to risk any of his lead by looking back to check. "Runs Fast knows the camp better than the Kiowa does," he said to himself. "We still have a chance to get away." Ahead of him, the Comanche boy dashed away from the fire. Trying to keep up with his friend, Sul followed him into the darkness.

Suddenly Runs Fast tripped over the tie rope of another pony and fell. Sul managed to jump over the rope, but the two of them lost precious seconds as the Comanche boy scrambled to regain his footing and avoid the hoofs of the frightened horse. Takes-Many-Scalps was right on their heels as Sul grabbed the other boy and pulled him down to safety in the shadows beside a solitary tepee. Hardly daring to breathe, they squatted there, leaning on their hands as their pursuer plunged after them. As the Kiowa rushed past, he almost stepped on Sul's right hand.

Just then someone threw more wood on the fire. The flames flared up, revealing the boys' hiding place. Another yell from Takes-Many-Scalps told them they had again been spotted.

"Come on," Runs Fast gasped, dragging Sul to his feet. "This way." Then they were running again, heading into an area where the tepees were pitched more closely together. A cluster of five lodges loomed before them, and for a brief moment they lost their pursuer in the darkness.

"Quick," the Comanche boy said over his shoulder, "under this tepee. Everyone is at the dance." He dropped to the ground and ducked under the raised side of the nearest lodge. Without question, Sul dived under the side of the tepee after him.

"I hope I'm all the way in," he said to himself, trying to feel for the side of the tepee in the darkness. One of his hands slapped what he thought was Runs Fast's face; then Runs Fast grabbed his arm and pulled him deeper into the tepee. His heart pounding in his ears, Sul joined the Indian boy on the owner's sleeping robe. He lay there beside his friend, trying to bring his heartbeat under control. Just outside the tepee, he heard Takes-Many-Scalps' light footsteps as the Kiowa ran up and halted.

"He's trying to figure out where we've gone," Sul told himself, tensing. "It won't take him long to guess we ducked into one of these tepees and come looking for us." Thinking they would have to take off running again, the boy began to ease himself up on one knee.

Outside, the footsteps turned and walked away. Takes-Many-Scalps had decided to check one of the other tepees first.

Sul sat up. Beside him, Runs Fast sighed softly and also started to rise. A faint noise behind them caused both boys to turn. In the darkness of the tepee Sul sensed rather than saw a tall, dark shape looming over them. Whether or not it held a knife he could not tell.

HEADING HOME

For an instant Sul's heart seemed to stand still. Then Runs Fast spoke softly but urgently in Comanche, and the dark figure gave a chuckle before answering in an old, cracked voice. With another laugh, the man sat down between the boys and the door of the tepee just as Takes-Many-Scalps came up outside.

Sul held his breath, wondering if the old man was going to betray them to the Kiowa. But the Comanche spoke sharply like an elder who has been rudely awakened. Takes-Many-Scalps answered angrily, as if demanding to know where they had gone, and the old man spoke to him again. Then, without entering the tepee, the Kiowa turned and walked away.

"Why did the old man hide us?" Sul whispered when at last it seemed safe to speak.

Runs Fast did not answer. Instead, the Indian boy turned over into the sleeping robe, and Sul felt the other boy's shoulders heave with laughter. "What's so funny?" he asked his friend.

Runs Fast brought himself under control before answering. "Big joke on Kiowa. Old-and-Wrinkled was once a great warrior but now is blind. I told him that we in trouble for mischief. He says boys will be boys and tells Kiowa the truth — that he did not see us." The Indian boy chuckled again. "He is always good to boys."

Sul relaxed and grinned. "Tell him thanks for his help. But if he really wants to be good to boys, he can think of some way of getting us safely back to He-Who-Sees-Far. I have no wish to meet the Kiowa and his knife again."

"Do not worry." Runs Fast sat up. "Old-and-Wrinkled shamed him — asked why a great warrior like him is angry at two boys. Kiowa will not bother us now."

There was no sign of the Kiowa anywhere when the boys ducked out of the old warrior's tepee a few minutes later. Sul half expected Takes-Many-Scalps to jump out at them again as they walked back to the fire, but nothing happened. When they joined Hanse Mason, the sergeant listened quietly as Sul related his and Runs Fast's adventure.

"The Seminoles have already got the Kickapoos on the warpath," Mason said when the boy had finished. "An' from what I've been able to learn from the elders here an' the visitin' Anadarkos, there's a war faction developin' in the other Comanche bands as well. It's headed by Buffalo Hump an' another chief called Horse Back. What you've found out just confirms what I'd heard."

"Thanks to Runs Fast," Sul said. "What about Chief Ketumse? Will he stay friendly?"

Mason nodded at Runs Fast who was sitting respectfully in the background while Sul made his report. "I've talked to the chief. Right now he an' most of his band want peace, but that could change. Game's gettin' scarce, an' he says it's time the Great Father in Washington comes up with some presents for the People if he don't want 'em raidin' the settlements. I told him I'd pass the word along."

"We have kept our promises to the white men — even without presents." Runs Fast spoke stiffly.

"An' so you have," the sergeant agreed, "except for maybe a

horse here an' there an' a sky-eyed boy who'd make a good warrior for the People. But you an' I both know that if some young braves from Ketumse's band decide to go on the war trail against the white man or even just raidin' our settlements on their own there ain't goin' to be much your chief can do about it."

"It is so," the Indian boy agreed.

Mason went on. "An' if enough of the warriors in this band decide on war, Chief Ketumse will have to go along with 'em or lose his headship. That or the band'll split. An' that's what's gettin' ready to happen now if Buffalo Hump gets his way."

Runs Fast looked down. "He-Who-Sees-Far speaks the truth," he said heavily.

Sul glanced from Mason to Runs Fast and then back again. He had thought that Indian chiefs had more control over their people than that, but he realized now he had been mistaken. "What do we do about it, Hanse?" he asked.

"The Bureau of Indian Affairs an' army headquarters in San Antone need to know what we've found out right away," the sergeant said. "A big handout of rations along with some other presents'd go a long ways toward helpin' keep the peace, but it'll take a while to get the government movin'. We'd better head for the settlements in the mornin' so I can report as soon as possible." He looked closely at Sul as though measuring the boy's disappointment. "Since I've talked to the Anadarkos, there won't be no need for us to visit José María's village. He's doin' what he can to keep the peace."

Sul waved this regret away. "That's all right," he said, "helping the frontier comes first." Then he frowned worriedly. "Hanse, we've got all those packhorses to take back. The Kiowa and the others could make trouble for us out on the plains."

Mason nodded at the boy. "I don't think he'll try anythin' now. Laughin' Boy an' Tall Horse have asked if they could ride with us to the river on our way to José María's village. Just in case I'll tell 'em we have to get on back, but that they can go with us as far as the military road. The three of us should be a match for the Kiowa an' his Seminole pals."

They rode away from Ketumse's village the next morning just after daybreak, Mason leading two of the packhorses while Laughing Boy and Tall Horse led the other three. Dr. Sturm, Runs Fast, and White Bull had seen them off, the Comanche boy even coming to the outskirts of the camp with them.

"Looks like you made a real friend," the sergeant said as Sul returned Runs Fast's wave. "An' I see you gave him your silk neckerchief."

"He admired it," Sul explained. "He said it was like my eyes." The boy turned to face the sergeant, who was riding beside him. "Hanse," he asked quietly, "do you think I'll ever get to see Runs Fast again?"

"Don't know, young'un. But over the years I've noticed that once my trail crosses somebody else's, it usually crosses again. Life's like that."

"I hope so," Sul said. For a few minutes he rode silently, staring between Saber's ears and thinking again of the friends he was leaving behind. Then he spotted the camp pony herd grazing at a distance and remembered the question he had wanted to ask the day before. "Hanse," he said, turning back to the sergeant, "did you ever steal horses when you were with the Comanches?"

Mason nodded. "I was a year or so older than Pete when I went on my third horse-stealin' raid with Gray Wolf's youngest nephew. The settlers killed him an' wounded me as I was tryin' to carry his body off. They would have killed me too, but old Miz Mason realized that I was white an' stopped 'em."

Sul had never heard this story before, for Hanse rarely spoke at length about his past, but now he wanted to know more. "What happened then?" he asked eagerly.

"She cared enough about me to treat my wounds an' nurse me back to health."

"Did you want to return to the Comanches when you got well?" the boy went on.

"By then I'd been around white folks enough to remember my pa an' ma, an' I didn't want to go back. Miz Mason was mighty good to me, an' I stayed with her till she died. Took her last name, too."

Sul considered this information. "You don't even remember your family name?" he asked finally in a small voice.

"Not a bit of it, young'un," Mason replied. "My ma called me 'Little Hans' so she must have been German. I think my pa was Irish. But I'll never know for sure."

The boy's face puckered in his distress. "That's awful — not to know your family name," he said. Again Sul rode in silence for a few minutes, thinking what it would mean to have no family identity. Suddenly the cabin in Waco seemed more homelike and desirable than it had in months. "I wouldn't have forgotten my ma and pa," he burst out finally.

"You're a lot older than I was when I was captured, Sully," Mason told him.

Sul squirmed embarrassedly at being misunderstood. "No, Hanse, I didn't mean that," he said, dropping his voice. "What I meant was that even if Laughing Boy and Tall Horse had carried me off where you couldn't find me, somehow I would have found a way to get back home."

"I thought you were runnin' away to live with the Anadarkos," Mason said innocently. "Wouldn't the Comanches have done just as well? Ketumse's band would have been glad to have you."

"Maybe for a while, but I wouldn't have stayed with them or the Anadarkos the rest of my life," Sul explained earnestly. "I would have gone home eventually."

The sergeant nodded shortly. "I know you would have, young'un," he agreed, his mouth twisting into a smile. "You'd stayed away from home just long enough to prove yourself to your pa — even though you don't want to see him again."

More embarrassed by Mason's understanding of his innermost feelings than he was by being misunderstood, Sul lowered his eyes back between Saber's ears and rode for a long time in silence.

About sunset on the second day of hard riding, Sul, Sergeant Mason, and the Comanche warriors caught their first glimpse of the military road running from Fort Gates to Fort Graham and then on to Fort Worth. Laughing Boy raised one braceleted arm and pointed. "We kept our word," he said to Sul and Mason in English. "We will turn back now."

"You have kept your word," the sergeant agreed. "We give you many thanks."

Sul grinned to himself. There had been no sign of the Seminoles or the Kiowa Takes-Many-Scalps. And although once they caught a glimpse of what looked like a Kickapoo war party in the distance, the Kickapoo warriors had thereafter avoided their group.

Laughing Boy turned then to Sul. "*Adios*, Little Sky Eyes," he said, smiling. "Takes-Many-Scalps says you are bad medicine. Still I would like you for my *tua*."

Sul leaned from his saddle to hold out his Colt. "I want you to have this," he said. "Wait and I will give you the bullet mold and everything that goes with it." He turned and dug into one of the sacks tied to his saddle for the other items.

Surprised, the Comanche took the weapon. "Why give me this?" he asked.

"Keep it to remember your almost *tua*," Sul said, handing over the case and other accessories. The boy smiled at the warrior. "I enjoyed seeing how the People live."

Laughing Boy's eyes gleamed. "Sky Eyes *muy generoso*. I will keep little pistol as he says."

Not wanting Tall Horse to feel left out, Sul took off his hunting knife and held it out to the other warrior. "This is for you,"
he said.

Laughing Boy chuckled and said something to his friend, and
Tall Horse took the gift. His hands made the sign for gratitude.
Both seemed pleased with their presents. And as the warriors
rode off, they both waved.

"I hope you don't mind that I gave away your gifts, Hanse,"
Sul said once the Comanches were out of hearing. "Somehow it
seemed like the right thing to do."

Mason tied the lead rope of the first of the three packhorses
he was leading securely to his saddle before answering.
"Young'un," he said finally, "you probably did more for good
relations with the Comanches by givin' those two them presents
than a troop of grownups could have done in a month of
Sundays. An' right now we need good relations." He handed the
boy the lead ropes of the other two horses.

"Do you think Tall Horse and Laughing Boy'll go on the
warpath?" Sul asked, dallying the rope of the first horse around
his saddle horn.

Mason shook his head. "Don't know, young'un. Right now
Ketumse's got his people in line, an' they've got their minds on
takin' Kickapoo scalps. But like I said earlier, that could change.
Thanks to your generosity, some of 'em at least will think twice
before takin' the war trail." The sergeant put his mount into a
trot. "Come on," he said. "We'll cut across country an' get on the
road before we stop for the night."

Sul turned Saber in beside the sergeant's horse. "Hanse," he
began slowly, as if something was puzzling him, "I've got a question. If the Comanches are friendly, why did you want damages
from them?"

"It's customary, young'un, in cases of honor."

Sul indicated the string of loaded packhorses trotting along
behind them. "Was your honor worth so much?" he asked.

Mason's eyes glinted. "Maybe mine wasn't, but Gray Wolf's sure was. He would have been shamed, Sully, if I hadn't asked for payment of some kind for what they'd done."

Sul considered this information. "I see," he said finally. "But why all this? I can understand the dried meat because we've eaten it, but five horses and fifteen buffalo robes? What are you going to do with all of them?"

To his surprise the sergeant laughed. "It's what *we're* goin' to do with 'em," he said. "Don't you see, young'un? We can sell them horses an' robes to start a stake for your later schoolin'. It won't be much at first, but you can keep addin' to it."

Sul blinked. "You mean you were willing to fight the Kiowa to get me a stake for my education?"

Mason nodded. "I'll go you one better," he said. "I'll match anythin' you can make on your own up to thirty dollars a year."

For a moment Sul was too overwhelmed to speak. Finally, though, he shook his head. "I can't let you do that, Hanse," he said regretfully. "I can't be beholden for something that important — even to you."

"Why not?" Mason asked. "I would have done it for my own son. An' if you're worried about what your pa will say, I'll talk him around if he cuts up rough. After all," the sergeant added humorously, "he won't be payin' for it."

At any other time, Sul would have recognized the humor of Mason's statement. Now, as he remembered what his father had said about not changing his mind, the old feeling of being trapped in the life of a farmer washed over him again. "I don't think that would make any difference to Pa," he said dully.

FLOOD AT BARTON'S FERRY

It was just getting dark when they went into camp. Sul rolled into his blanket early but was too troubled at first to sleep. "Tomorrow we'll reach Fort Graham, and from there it's only forty miles on to Waco," he told himself gloomily. Soon, too soon, his adventure would be over and he would be home again, having to face his father and the consequences of running away. "If only Pa would listen to Hanse and let him help me get my schooling," he said to himself, sighing. "Then maybe I would still have a chance to become an officer someday." With another sigh, deeper than the one before, Sul hitched his blanket higher on one shoulder, folded his arms, and once again sought sleep.

Sometime before dawn, he awakened to find Mason moving around their camp.

"Trouble, Hanse?" the boy asked, sitting up. He reached for his rifle. For an instant he regretted giving away his revolver. "Is it the Kickapoos again?"

The sergeant's voice was reassuring. "Line of bad thunderstorms to the north an' west of us," he answered. Behind him a faint flash of lightning lit the sky. "Comanche Peak would have been right in the middle of 'em."

Sul yawned. "That's miles away," he said. "How long until dawn?"

"Only about an hour — two at the most. Go back to sleep." As Mason spoke, Sul could hear a low rumble of distant thunder. Around him the horses began to stamp and sidle uneasily.

"No, I'm awake now." Getting to his feet, Sul went to check on Saber's picket rope. It was securely fastened, and for a few minutes he stood watching the lightning and listening to the faraway growl of thunder. "Do you think it'll come this way?" he asked.

Mason studied the sky before answering. "Might go around," he said finally, "but I don't think so." He turned to the boy. "Since you're awake, let's break camp an' head for Barton's Ferry. With any luck we can be across the Brazos an' back at the post for early mess."

Working by touch rather than sight, Sul collected his horse equipment and smoothed his saddle blanket over Saber's back. "Hanse, do you really think Pa would let me pay for my own schooling?" he asked, pausing in lifting his saddle into place.

Mason halted in his own preparations. Once again his voice was reassuring in the darkness. "If he didn't, young'un, you could wait until you're old enough, an' then do it on your own," he said quietly. "I ain't one to advise insubordination, but this is one time I'd say it was justified."

They reached Barton's Ferry on the Brazos a little after eight that morning after riding about daybreak through a downpour which lasted for some time.

"Look," Sul said as they rode up to the ferry landing leading their string of loaded packhorses. "We've just missed the ferry." The ferryman, Mr. Barton, was starting across with a full load of one man on horseback and another with a two-mule hack. There were also several people standing in the road above the landing — Mrs. Barton and her two children, and her mother, the Widow Oakes from Waco.

"Hi, Sul!" As the ferry got under way, Charley Oakes waved widely from the rear of the boat. "I didn't think I'd see you here," his friend called.

"Hi, Charley." Sul returned the wave. Even from where he and Hanse sat their horses, the boy could see there had been a considerable rise on the river. The muddy water ran strong and fast, and while he watched, several large tree limbs floated past with a rush.

"Look at the river, Hanse." Sul motioned toward the Brazos. "Pa told me to be extra careful crossing when it looks like that."

"Your pa told you right," the sergeant agreed, leaning his elbows on his saddle pommel. "From the looks of it, there's high water on the way after that rain last night."

Their voices carried, and Mrs. Barton, holding her son and daughter by the hand, walked across the muddy road to meet them. Her mother followed.

"Sergeant Mason — " the ferryman's wife began, recognizing the noncommissioned officer. Then she stopped and stared at the boy riding beside him. "Sul Ross, what are you doing here? Mother said the news from Waco last week was that you had run away."

Mason touched his hat to the two women. "'Morning, Miz Barton — Miz Oakes. Sully's been out on the plains with me," he said by way of explanation. "Looks like the river's on a rise," he went on.

Elizabeth Barton nodded. She released her children's hands. "Josh," she said to her little boy, "take your sister back to the house." Once the pair had started back to the cabin, Mrs. Barton faced the newcomers. "I begged Al not to try to cross now," she said fretfully, "but those two men insisted on being taken to the other side right away." She looked meaningfully at her mother. "And my little brother got on with them."

Mrs. Oakes frowned at her daughter. "Do you think there is any dan — " she began, but she never finished her question.

From upriver came a deep rumbling followed by a crashing, bellowing roar like a thousand wild bulls on the rampage. They all looked that way.

"Hanse!" Sul yelled, pointing upstream. "Look at the river! It's just like Pa said!"

As they watched, a muddy red wall of water charged down the Brazos, pushing uprooted trees and other debris ahead of it.

"Al, watch out!" Mrs. Barton cried.

Before the party in the road could move, the wave struck the ferry side on, flipped it over, and dumped all on board into the raging floodwaters. The women screamed.

"Charley!" Sul loosed the lead rope from his saddle horn and kicked Saber into a run for the landing. Beside him, Mason also sprang into action. Out in mid-stream four heads bobbed in the muddy waters as the ferryman and his passengers were swept downstream.

At the landing, Sul flung himself off Saber's back and grabbed up a coil of rope hanging on the tie-up post. He was scrambling back into the saddle when Mason came charging up.

"Hanse, we've got to save Charley!" he cried.

"One of 'em grabbed a plank an' him an' the boy are hangin' onto it," Mason answered, leaning from his saddle to take the rope from him. "I'tl get 'em to shore. It's Barton an' the other one we need to worry about." The sergeant vaulted from the saddle and ran down the bank to the water's edge.

"Mr. Barton!" Sul suddenly remembered the ferryman. He stared downstream and spotted Barton's balding head still bobbing in the flood. The man was thrashing around, struggling weakly to keep his head above water. "I'll go after him!" the boy yelled over his shoulder, reining his horse around. "Saber's faster than Chief!"

"You may not be able to get him out!" Mason called after him.

"I've got to try!" Ducking low in his saddle, Sul weaved Saber among the trees and underbrush growing along the river, trying to keep that balding head in sight. A branch tore off his hat and scratched his face, and he bent lower over the roan's mane. When Sul reached a cleared area, he put the little horse into as fast a pace as he dared.

On they raced. Ahead of him the river made a small loop, and he cut his horse across the neck of land. When he spotted the ferryman again, he was alongside the man floundering in the water.

"Mr. Barton," Sul yelled, "angle yourself to this side! I'll try to catch you at the next bend!" There was no way of knowing if the ferryman had heard him over the roar of the water, and Sul could only plunge Saber forward.

As he hoped, the river swung to the south in another bend. Ahead of the flood victim now, Sul jumped Saber over a log, threw himself from the saddle, and pounded toward the river-bank. On the way he stooped and snatched up a fallen tree limb to drag it forward with him.

"Mr. Barton," he screamed, leaning over the river bank to shove the branch out into the stream of the Brazos, "catch hold!"

He caught a glimpse of a pale, strained face and wild eyes as the ferryman was swept toward him. The man made a weak, unsuccessful grab at the far end of the limb, missed by inches, and went under in a swirl of water.

"Mr. Barton!" Sul shrieked, dropping to his knees and trying to push the branch farther out into the water. "If you can, grab hold!"

There was no answer, no sign of the drowning man. Stunned, Sul hesitated for an instant. Then he dropped the branch, jumped back up, and sprinted downstream along the riverbank looking for him. Suddenly the ground beneath his feet, undercut by the flood, gave way, and he found himself dropping feet first into the raging waters.

TO THE RESCUE

Sul screamed as he dropped. As he fell, a sturdy tree root growing out from a nearby oak nearly struck him in the face, but he was able to grab it as he fell past and hang on. Still, he hit the water, sinking armpit deep as he swung at arms' length from the root.

Immediately the flood waters jerked at him, threatening to wrench his handhold loose. Gasping at the cold, the boy tried to pull himself up, but his clothes and boots weighted him down. For the first time since the flood began he felt real fear.

Somehow he fought it down. "Got to kick my boots off," Sul told himself. He held the heel of one boot down with the side of the other and managed to pull it off. Before he could shed the other boot, though, he glanced back and saw a large tree limb barreling down on him.

He twisted out of the way as much as possible, but the end of the limb still struck him a solid blow before the branch slid on past. Sul felt a sharp pain in his left shoulder, so sharp that it took his breath away, and then his left hand lost its grip. Slowly his left arm sank to his side and hung uselessly.

Sul set his teeth against the pain and held on, gripping all the tighter with his right hand. "Got to hang on," he told himself. "Hanse will come looking for me. He's just got to."

He seemed to wait an eternity. Minutes passed. The cold waters tore at him, pulling his legs out from under him and threatening to jerk loose his unsteady hold. "Hanse!" Sul yelled. "Hurry, please!"

There was no answer but the roar of the water. Sul swallowed hard and concentrated on holding to the root. More time went by. Now it seemed his hand was getting numb. Soon, perhaps, he would lose his grip and be swept away, just like Mr. Barton. Sul shuddered at the thought of drowning. "Hanse!" he yelled again.

This time he heard Mason's voice over the rush of the flood. "Hanse, over here!" Sul cried, twisting in the current as the muddy waters battered at him. Surely they were higher now on his back and chest than they had been when he first fell in. "And hurry!" he screamed.

In reply, Sul heard a crash of underbrush above him on the river bank and then the approach of running feet. "Sully, where are you?" Mason shouted overhead.

"Down here, in the water!" Sul yelled back. "Hurry, Hanse! The water's rising!"

Mason appeared then on the river bank above his head. The sergeant had a coil of rope around one shoulder. "Reach up an' grab on with your other hand," he ordered.

"I can't," Sul told him. "I've hurt my arm."

"Don't let go, then." The sergeant lay down on his stomach and stretched out his arm to try to grasp Sul's wrist, but his reach wasn't long enough.

"Hurry," Sul begged. "I — I can't hold on much longer."

"You can," Mason told him, his face unusually tense. "That's an order, soldier!" He shuffled the rope off his shoulder, found one end, and stretched enough to pass a long loop around the boy's right wrist. "I'm goin' to get you out," he promised, tying a knot and pulling it tightly against the boy's wrist, so tightly that

Sul almost cried out at the pain. "When I give the word, you let go. You might go under, but I won't let you drown, young'un."

Sul looked up into the sergeant's face. Mason's expression was even more strained than before. "He's afraid for me," Sul thought in surprise. This realization made him smile lopsidedly in an effort to reassure his friend. "I know you won't — Uncle Comanche," he said.

Mason's mouth twisted. "Let go!" he ordered.

Sul released his hold. Down he sank, the muddy waters of the Brazos closing over his head, but the rope binding his wrist held. He felt a powerful jerk and then began to rise. Before he knew it, he was lying on the river bank while Mason bent over him, feeling his left arm and shoulder.

"Hanse," Sul gasped as river water ran down his face, "is Charley safe?"

Mason pushed something back into place in Sul's shoulder before answering. "Safe as can be," he said. "He's probably tucked up in bed now with his ma hangin' over him."

"And the others?" Sul wanted to know. Now that the chill from the water was subsiding, he could really feel the pain of his injury.

"They were saved too. What about Barton?"

Sul closed his eyes momentarily at the memory. "He drowned in front of me. I put out a branch to him, Hanse, but he couldn't grab it. Do you think we can find his body?"

"There ain't goin' to be no 'we' about it, young'un," the sergeant said, making a sling out his bandana and putting the boy's arm into it. "You've broken your collarbone, an' I'm takin' you straight back to the ferry so we can get it set."

"But Mrs. Barton — " Sul protested. "She'll want his body recovered."

"If Barton's drowned, then his body can wait," Mason answered. "Right now you're more important. Lay quiet till I get back — I've got to go to my horse."

Sul lay where he was in the grass of the river bank, too weak to move and too numb to care as the sergeant strode off. In his imagination, once more he saw Mr. Barton's look of terror as the drowning man grabbed for the end of the branch and missed. Suddenly a wave of cold swept over him, and he found himself shivering violently. He wanted to cry, too. "Soldiers don't cry," Sul told himself fiercely, fighting back the tears.

He was still shivering as Mason returned with a blanket. "Hanse, what's wrong with me?" he asked, his teeth chattering. "I'm not afraid — honest, I'm not. At least not now. And besides, it's all over."

"I know you're not afraid, young'un," the sergeant replied. "You fought a good action." He knelt beside the boy and half raised him to wrap him in the blanket. "This is the cold that follows injury an' pain. It's why I've got to get you back to Miz Barton's — pronto. Let's just hope she's got a pot of coffee or a kettle of soup on the fire." He gathered the youngster into his arms.

"I can walk," Sul protested, but Mason paid him no heed. He carried the boy to his sorrel and lifted him into his own saddle.

"A good officer knows when to hand over command," the sergeant said, mounting behind Sul and leaning from his horse's back to take Saber's reins. "Right now you're out of action."

For the moment Sul did not answer; the movement had made him dizzy, and he was grateful to be riding double. The world was spinning as Mason put his horse into a walk.

Sul clutched the sergeant's arm to keep from falling. "Hanse, I've got to find my hat — Pa will be angry if I've lost it as well as my boot."

"I'll look for it later," Mason promised, urging his horse forward. "But I don't think your pa's goin' to have that much to say about you losin' it."

"I hope so," Sul said, wishing the world would stop turning around. At last it did so, but as Chief stepped out, the boy found

himself having to bite his lips against the growing pain of movement.

"Hurts, don't it?" Mason asked. "After I get you to Miz
Barton's I can look for somethin' to ease the pain, but right now
you're goin' to have to just take it like a good soldier."

Sul nodded. "How will I tell Mrs. Barton about her husband?"
he asked worriedly.

"Tell her what you told me about him drownin' in front of
you," Mason said, settling the boy more comfortably in the
crook of one arm.

"Hanse, I can't." Sul shivered again at the memory, and
Mason wrapped him more closely in the blanket.

"Young'un, you've got to. She needs to know."

"But I may be wrong," Sul protested. "Maybe Mr. Barton didn't
drown after all." His teeth chattered. "At least I hope he didn't."

"Sully, you've got to tell her the truth," Mason answered,
guiding the sorrel around the trees growing on the riverbank.
"It'd be better for her to think he was dead an' have him turn up
alive than for you to mislead her into thinkin' he's alive when
he's more than likely drowned. Miz Barton's a strong woman,
just like your ma. She can take it."

This mention of Mrs. Ross made Sul's eyes fill, and he dashed
the tears away with his right hand. His father could have been
the one who drowned, and his mother would now be what Mrs.
Barton was — a widow. His brothers and sisters — and himself
— would now be fatherless, like Mrs. Barton's children. "I would
like to see Ma again," he whispered. "And Pa."

"I thought you never wanted to see your pa again," Mason
answered, holding him closer. "At least that's what you said the
day I came up with you — an' several times since."

"I know," Sul said wearily and sighed. That day out on the
plains seemed far away now. "I've changed my mind, Hanse.
When Laughing Boy told me I'd never have to see Pa again I
realized that I wanted to — I just didn't want to admit it. And I

am grateful to Pa for all he taught me about getting along with the Indians. It's really come in handy the last few days."

"Sounds like you've done some growin' up this trip, young'un," Mason said. They had entered a cleared area, and he urged his sorrel into a running walk. All Sul could do was grit his teeth and hang on.

Mrs. Barton and her mother were on the watch for them. The two women hurried out onto the gallery when they rode up to the cabin. "Al?" the younger woman asked anxiously. "Did you see him, Sul?"

Wincing, the boy sat up to make his report. "I'm-I'm sorry, Mrs. Barton, but your husband drowned," he said. "I-I saw him go under and not come back up." To his dismay, his teeth began chattering again.

Mrs. Barton did not cry. Instead, she seemed to give herself a little shake and turn to more important business at hand. "You're hurt," she said.

"Broke his collarbone." Mason dismounted and lifted the boy down from his saddle. "If it's all right with you, Miz Barton, I'd like to bring him inside. He's wet an' chilled. We need to get him warm an' dry fast."

"There's a fresh pot of coffee," Mrs. Oakes said, taking charge. "I'll get a cup while you bring him inside. Show the sergeant where to put him, Lizabeth — in bed with Charley will be fine. Then get one of Al's shirts for him to sleep in and some cloth for bandaging. And he'll need a better sling than that bandana."

Sometime later, Sul awakened from a nightmare about drowning and sat up in bed with a shudder. He felt hot and feverish, and his injury throbbed painfully. On the other side of him, Charley Oakes slept soundly after his ordeal in the water.

"What is it, Sul?" Mrs. Barton rose from a rocking chair across the room and came to his bedside. Her voice was calm, comforting. "Were you having a bad dream?"

Sul nodded, still too shaken to speak, and looked around. "Where's Hanse?" he asked finally.

"He and Mr. Jackson have gone downstream to look for Al's body. Then he said he had to report to the fort, even if it meant going the long way round to the Waco ferry and back."

Sul nodded again. "What we learned from Chief Ketumse," he said. By then he had noticed that her eyes were red with weeping, and, for the first time, he began openly to cry.

"What's wrong, child?" she asked gently, putting an arm around him.

"I — I tried to save your husband, but I couldn't," the boy sobbed. "But I tried, honest I did. I just couldn't do it."

"Sergeant Mason explained that," Mrs. Barton replied. "He said you were the gamest young'un he'd ever run across."

Ignoring this praise, Sul struggled to bring his crying under control. At last he succeeded. "I might have died today!" he said, shuddering again. "If Hanse hadn't gotten me out I would have drowned."

"But you didn't, Sul. Thank heaven your life was spared." Mrs. Barton felt his forehead. "You've got fever. Does your shoulder hurt?"

Suddenly Sul felt like one big ache. "I want Ma," he whispered.

Mrs. Barton hugged him closer. "I'm sorry, but your ma's a long way off. Mother and I will take care of you." She turned and spoke over her shoulder to Mrs. Oakes, who had just come into the room. "Ma, bring that cup of willow bark tea Sergeant Mason told us to brew. I think it's time Sul had a dose."

Mrs. Oakes walked over from the fireplace, carrying the cup. "I'm sure the sergeant will send word to your folks," she told Sul. "Why, by this time tomorrow your father could be here."

"No, not Pa!" Sul said wildly. "I don't feel like seeing Pa so soon." It was all he could do to keep from crying again. "I ran away — left Ma in the lurch, like Hanse said. I'm sorry, but I don't want to see Pa — at least not yet."

"But of course you'll want to see your pa — " the Widow Oakes began, but a glance from her daughter cut her off short.

"Whatever you've done, Sul, your parents will be glad to learn you are safe," Mrs. Barton said soothingly. "Now drink this tea and go back to sleep. You'll feel better tomorrow no matter who comes to see you."

The boy nodded. After he had choked down the bitter tea and had been tucked back into bed, Sul realized that Hanse would make it a point to go by Waco and tell his father all that had happened. He also realized that for the present he was too tired to care.

A DOOR OPENS

T he next evening Sul was sitting in a rocking chair in Mrs. Barton's living area watching Charley play with a top when he heard a solitary horseman ride up outside. Immediately Mrs. Barton went to the door. Charley followed her.

"Good evening, Captain Ross," Sul heard her greet the new-comer.

"'Evening, Mrs. Barton." Shap Ross' voice reached his son's ears. "Sorry to hear about your husband. Let me know if there's anything I can do for you."

"Thank you," she said. "You'll find Sul inside, but you need to know that he shouldn't be moved home until that collarbone knits."

"I don't doubt that you've taken good care of him," Shapley Ross replied. "We'd like him at home in Waco, but I'm sure he's in good hands here."

"The very best," Mrs. Barton answered. "Go on in."

Sul sat up straighter in the rocking chair as his father came into the cabin. "Hanse told me how you tried to save Mr. Barton," Shapley Ross began. "I'm proud of you, son, but it's only what I would have expected from you or Pete."

"Yes, Pa." At any other time, Sul would have beamed at this praise. Right now the boy knew he had confessions to make, and he didn't know how his father would take them. Sul swallowed hard. "I — I lost one of my boots in the flood," he began uncertainly. "My hat too, but Hanse found it for me."

"We'll get you another pair," his father promised. He didn't seem unduly concerned about the expense.

Thus encouraged, Sul went on. "I'm sorry I ran away."

Shap Ross ignored his apology. "Most boys run away one time or another," he said and then frowned. "Hanse told me that you ran away because you wanted more schooling — that you want to go to military school like Pete. Is that right?"

Sul nodded.

"Son, don't you see I can't afford to send both of you back east?" Shap Ross spoke earnestly. "We're getting ready to marry off both your older sisters this year, and the farm's not producing good yet. On top of that, I have to hire help for the farm and for the ferry. I can only send one of you to secondary school, and Pete is the oldest. It's only right that he should be the one to go."

"You said you weren't going to send me to school beyond this year — " Sul said bleakly. He no longer cared who saw his misery.

"You've already had four years of formal schooling which is more than I got." Shapley Ross reached out and patted his son's unbandaged shoulder awkwardly. "It's Mervin's turn to start school this fall. He's sickly and needs to learn to read and write so he can clerk for somebody and not have to work hard."

Overwhelmed by unhappiness, Sul could only look at his father. Ross squatted on his heels beside the rocking chair, bringing himself as much as possible down to his son's level.

"Please understand, son. I don't have anything against you getting more education — but it's just not possible now. And we need your help at the farm."

"But I wanted to be a soldier too," Sul whispered. "Didn't I prove I could be?"

Shap Ross did not directly answer his son's question. "Hanse told me about your adventures, and you have had quite a time," he said, "but Pete's going to be our soldier." He laughed nervously, not seeming to notice the hurt in Sul's eyes. "There are a lot of things you can do instead, like being a ranger if the need arises. And just remember there are plenty of self-made men in Texas. You don't need more education to get ahead here."

Sul squeezed his eyes tightly shut to keep from crying. He suddenly felt weak and shaky. More than that, he realized that he hadn't been successful in proving himself to his father. "In spite of all my adventures nothing's changed," he told himself. He was still the unimportant middle child, the one to give way for the benefit of those older and younger in the family.

The boy sighed. "I'm no nearer becoming a soldier than before," he said to himself. "In fact, I'm farther away." More than that, Hanse's idea for him to pay for his own schooling in the future would mean nothing if he didn't get the chance to continue his studies now. "If Pa puts me to work on the farm, I'll never escape — never," Sul told himself gloomily.

He was so busy considering the bleakness of such a future that at first he didn't notice that Mrs. Barton had come back into the cabin.

"Just a minute, Captain Ross," Sul heard her say. "Did you mean what you said just now about me letting you know if there was anything you could do for me?"

Sul opened his eyes to see his father looking startled, as if he wondered at her questioning his word.

"Of course I did, Mrs. Barton. Is there something?" Shapley Ross asked, getting back to his feet.

"As you know," she said, "my late husband had the contract for operating the ferry here on the military road between Fort Gates and Fort Graham. In fact, you helped him set it up."

Shapley Ross nodded, and Mrs. Barton went on. "Well, Al's gone now, but I'd like to keep the contract — and the income from the ferry — if I could."

"That's understandable," Sul's father said. "Do you need someone to work the ferry?"

"Yes," Mrs. Barton answered. "That's where I need your help. It will take us a while to get back into operation again, but when we do, I'll need someone to run the ferry for me."

"If you want, I'll find you someone in Waco and send them out here," the frontiersman promised.

Mrs. Barton looked past the elder Ross and smiled at Sul before replying. When she did speak her words surprised them both. "No," she said, "that won't be necessary. I want you to hire Sul out to me to operate the ferry for us. Not only will I pay you for his work, but I'll tutor him along with my brother and my own children." Again she smiled at the boy. "I can even start you in Latin, if you like, Sul."

Sul's heart leaped at this chance to go on with his studies. Gratitude to Mrs. Barton flooded his soul. "If I do that, maybe I can get my secondary schooling some day," he said to himself. "More than that, with Hanse just across the river, I'll be able to see him a lot more often." Hopefully, Sul looked to his father. Everything depended on him.

"If you pay me for Sul's hire," Shap Ross said, thinking out loud, "then I can pay someone to work out at the farm. A boy Sul's age can't do the work of a full hand yet, anyway." He rubbed his chin thoughtfully with one forefinger while Sul waited, hardly daring to breathe. "And he might as well be working here and getting the schooling he's so set on as mulligrubbing around home or trying to run away again," his father went on. Shap Ross suddenly stood. "All right," he said, "I'll do it. He'll have to go back to Waco soon, though. His mother will want to see him before he moves out here."

"That will be fine," Mrs. Barton agreed. "Sul will need his clothes, boots, books — and his horse. I'll be glad to provide free stabling."

Shapley Ross frowned as though reconsidering. "I guess Sul

can keep Saber here," he said finally. "The roan's too small for Pete to race, and Mervin's not old enough. Maybe Hanse can set up some match races for him over at Fort Graham." He shook his head slightly at his son. "I warn you, Mrs. Barton — Sul's getting to be a handful. This last escapade of his proved that."

"I can handle him," Mrs. Barton said positively. "Besides," she added, "Sergeant Mason will be at the fort across the river in case I need help. I think the two of us can keep him in line."

Sul turned to face the wall, afraid to let his father see his happiness at this unexpected door which had opened for him. Suddenly life looked a lot more hopeful, even if his father was planning to hire him out like a servant.

Again a feeling of gratitude to Mrs. Barton filled his heart. If she wanted someone to operate the ferry, he would work like two boys for the privilege of continuing his studies. And as for his own mother — someday Ma would be proud of him.

"I'll show you, Pa," Sul vowed under his breath as the grownups behind him began discussing wages, board, and other less interesting matters. "Thanks to Hanse I'll get my secondary schooling, if I have to pay for it myself. And I *will* be a soldier someday — just you wait and see."

LAWRENCE SULLIVAN "SUL" ROSS

Lawrence Sullivan Ross (better known to his contemporaries and to history as Sul Ross) was one of the most popular citizens of nineteenth-century Texas. His influence in Texas lasts until the present day.

Sul Ross was born in Bentonsport, Iowa, in 1838, the second son and fourth child of Shapley Prince Ross and Catherine Fulkerson Ross, both from Missouri. Through his father, Sul was related to presidents George Washington and Zachary Taylor. When he was a year old, his family came to Texas, settling in Milam County which was still the Indian frontier. Twice during his formative years Sul was in the hands and at the mercy of hostile Indians. Although his early goal in life was to be an Indian fighter like his father, it is possible he had military ambitions as well. His father apparently had them for Sul's older brother, Peter F. Ross, sending him to military school in New York state.

In 1849 the family moved to Waco, where Shap Ross became a ferry operator and land owner. The following year Sul went to live with Mrs. Elizabeth Barton, widow of the owner of Barton's Ferry on the Brazos River at Fort Graham. How long he lived with Mrs. Barton is not known, but he was to attribute much of his later success in life to her interest and influence.

Despite his frontier upbringing, young Ross realized the need for more education and in 1856 entered Baylor University. The next year, after spending some time in Young County where he met and learned to admire Robert E. Lee, then of the Second Cavalry, Sul transferred to the Wesleyan University in Florence, Alabama.

Ross' first military command came during his junior year when he was nineteen. That summer Sul arrived from Alabama at the Brazos Indian Reservation, where his father was special agent, in time to take command of 125 Caddo, Waco, Tonkawa, Anadarko, and Delaware warriors who were preparing to cooperate with U.S. troops in a strike against the Comanche homeland. During the ensuing campaign, Sul was severely wounded but won the praise of regular army officers who offered him a career in the U.S. Army. Ross declined the offer and returned to college.

Back in Texas following his graduation, he joined state troops in defense of the frontier. While commanding a company of rangers in December of 1860, Ross led an expedition against Peta Nocona's Comanche raiders. During this campaign, he recovered Cynthia Ann Parker from captivity and returned her to her family, an action which won him much popularity at the time.

With the coming of the War Between the States, Sul Ross resigned from the rangers. However, he put off enlisting in the Confederate Army until September 1861, acting in the meantime as a state peace commissioner to various Indian tribes and marrying his childhood sweetheart, Lizzie Tinsley. Once he joined the Sixth Texas Cavalry, he rose from private to brigadier general, winning the respect of his men and the praise of his superiors on 135 battlefields from Arkansas to Georgia. Although he was never wounded during the war, sickness, strain, and overwork took their toll, and the end of the war found the young general in Texas trying to regain his health.

Sul Ross spent the next eight years farming near Waco with his wife and family. In 1873 the citizens of his county desperately needed a brave and energetic sheriff, and former General Ross was their choice for the job. Resigning after two eventful years, Ross served in the constitutional convention where he helped write the present constitution of Texas and urged needed reforms. Service as constitutional delegate gave him a reputation for skill in public office, and in 1880 he was elected state senator. From the senate it was easy to advance to the governorship; he was elected in 1886 and served until 1891. During his time in office the new capitol was dedicated and many state services including education were strengthened.

Throughout his life Sul Ross had been interested in education, and when he left Austin he stepped into the presidency of the troubled Texas A.& M. College. By the time of his sudden death in 1898 the suffering institution was once more stable and growing.

As an editorial in the *Dallas Morning News* stated after his death, "It has been the lot of few men to be of such great service to Texas as Sul Ross. . . . Throughout his life he has been closely connected with the public welfare, and . . . discharged every duty imposed upon him with diligence, ability, honesty and patriotism."

GLOSSARY

barlow knife — A single-bladed pocket knife.

hickory shirt — Hickory, a sturdy cotton fabric woven to have diagonal ribs, was so-called because of its long-wearing capabilities.

parole — A military term meaning the promise (from French for "word of honor") of a prisoner of war not to try to escape or, if released, not to take up arms again against his captors.

paterollers — In plantation times, the patrol of slave owners who enforced the community's regulations for slaves.

savvy — A slang term derived from Spanish meaning, "Do you know?" or "Understand?"

terrapin — A tortoise or turtle.

throatlatch — The strap on a bridle which goes under the horse's throat and holds the bridle in place.

wamus — On the southern frontier, an ankle-length shirt worn as the only garment of little boys until they received their first trousers.

SELECTED READINGS

Benner, Judith Ann. *Sul Ross: Soldier, Statesman, Educator*. College Station: Texas A&M University Press, 1983.

Bolton, Paul. *Governors of Texas*. Corpus Christi: Caller-Times Publishing Company, 1947.

Conger, Roger N., et al. *Rangers of Texas*. Waco: Texian Press, 1969.

DeShields, James T. *They Sat in High Places: The Presidents and Governors of Texas*. San Antonio: Naylor Company, 1940.

"Lawrence Sullivan Ross," Walter Prescott Webb and H. Bailey Carroll, eds., *The Handbook of Texas*. 2 vols. Austin: The Texas State Historical Association, 1952. Vol. 2, pp. 506-507.

McKay, Seth Shepard. "Lawrence Sullivan Ross," Allen Johnson and Dumas Malone, eds., *Dictionary of American Biography*. 21 vols. New York: Charles Scribner's Sons, 1928-37. Vol. 26, pp. 179-80.

Shuffler, R. Henderson. *Son, Remember* . . . College Station: Texas A&M University, 1951.

The Author

Judith Ann Benner is librarian at Bethesda Christian Institute, the private school where she has taught for fifteen years. Her interest in Lawrence Sullivan Ross has led her to complete a biography of Ross and Lone Star Rebel, a juvenile historical novel about a fourteen-year-old boy in Sul Ross' Sixth Texas Cavalry. Presently, Dr. Benner is working on two more juvenile historical novels about the Texas frontier.